"Our Day Will Come"

An MM Gay Romance

Zachary Holland

This book is intended for Adults (ages 18+) only. The contents may be offensive to some readers. It may contain graphic language, explicit sexual content, and adult situations. May contain scenes of unprotected sex. Please do not read this book if you are offended by content as mentioned above or if you are under the age of 18. Please educate yourself on safe sex practices before making potentially life-changing decisions about sex in real life.

This story is a work of fiction. Names, characters, businesses, places, events and incidents are the products of the author's imagination or used in a fictitious manner and are not to be construed as real. Any resemblance to actual persons, living or dead, or actual events is purely coincidental. Products or brand names mentioned are trademarks of their respective holders or companies. The cover uses licensed images and are shown for illustrative purposes only. Any person(s) that may be depicted on the cover are simply models.

Edition v1.00 (2022.01.24)

Special thanks to the volunteer readers who helped with proofreading. Thank you so much for your support.

Chapter One

Melissa had always been beautiful, but she had never been more beautiful than one day in particular. She had called John and asked him to come over immediately. Whenever she got highly emotional it was always difficult to tell whether she was excited or distraught, at least over the phone, so John was in two minds about whether to be laughing or crying. When she opened the door she flung her arms around him and he still wasn't entirely sure which way the coin was going to fall. She was everything a woman should be; soft and loving and kind. Her hair was long and lustrous, her skin smooth and supple. She had an effervescent glow about her and John had always been jealous. The two of them had been as close as any two people could ever be. The love they shared was deep and pure, borne from a childhood bond that had lasted well into adulthood and that both of them were sure would last until they took their dying breaths as well. John had never counted on anyone as much as he counted on Melissa, and now he wondered if it was her turn to count on him.

He closed the door behind him and entered her apartment, which always smelled of vanilla. She had a strange look on her face, as though she was holding all the emotion in the world in her features and it would only take one moment for them to come pouring out in a torrent.

"I'm kind of worried to ask you what's happened," John said warily, ready to open his arms if she needed comfort.

"It's nothing bad," she reassured him. They sank down to the couch. She flashed him a smile. "It's just that I can't believe this is actually happening."

"It's about Ryan, isn't it?" John asked.

Melissa nodded and blinked a few times, as though she was blinking away tears. John wore concern upon his face, and he wondered if it was as good news as she thought. His heart clenched with fear as he had lived through the drama of her relationship alongside her, he had held her when she shuddered with sorrow, he had been angry with her when she ranted about something that Ryan had done, and he had worried with her when they spoke about the future.

Now he had to be happy with her, but he found that harder than it should have been because of everything that had come before.

"He finally did it John. He asked me, and now I have to ask you something to. Will you be my man of honor?"

John was silent for a few moments. Did that mean what he thought it meant? No... he had written off Ryan a while back. He thought it had only been a matter of time before they were on the outs as Ryan never seemed like he was going to commit.

"Wait... he asked you to marry him?"

"Yes!" Melissa exclaimed, nodding furiously, a wide smile beaming on her face. John couldn't remember the last time she had been this happy, but he couldn't just forget about all the times she had been on the brink of despair either.

"Are you sure this is what you want?" John asked.

The smile fell from her face. She furrowed her brow and gave him a withering stare. "Of course this is what I want! I've been wanting him to ask me this for ages!"

"I know... I just thought that after all you'd been through maybe this is something you need to be careful about."

Melissa rolled her eyes. "I don't need to be careful right now John, and I don't need you to be worried for me. I just need you to be happy."

"I am, if you are. I just want to make sure that I'm doing my due diligence," he said.

Melissa calmed somewhat and placed her hand on his. "I appreciate that, and I'm sorry for snapping at you. But I am happy. This is what I want. It's what we both want."

"It's just that I thought you two were fighting a lot. I thought he didn't want to get married. I'm sorry, I don't mean to be a downer or cast doubt on this, I'm just trying to process it. It's big news," John said, careful to make sure Melissa knew that he wasn't just trying to downplay her good news for no reason. It was all a whirl in his mind.

"It is," she agreed. "To be honest I'm still trying to process it myself. The fact is that he just changed his mind."

"Just like that? I wasn't sure Ryan was the type."

"I know we've had our problems in the past, but somehow we've always got through them and that means something, doesn't it?"

"Did he tell you why he changed his mind?" John asked, preferring not to answer her question. He was hardly the man that should go about lecturing other people about their relationships when he couldn't hang onto a man of his own.

"We were just talking about things and it was nice for it to not turn into an argument again. We actually spoke about our feelings and he told me why he was scared about getting married."

"Which is because...?"

Melissa shrugged. "Just basically that most of the people he knows who have gotten married have also gotten a divorce, and that he doesn't think it's that important to declare our love to people. He'd rather keep it between us. Which I get and everything, but then I told him why it's important to me and my family, and how I really want to get married before my grandparents die because I know they'd love it. And I'd love it too I mean, it's a once in a lifetime thing, isn't it? At least it should be. Plus there's the fact that I just love the idea of committing so fiercely to someone, to putting my trust in them and the relationship. So we talked about this for hours and then eventually he just said 'ok'."

"Just as easy as that?"

"Yeah. He said that he had never really thought about why it was so important to me before, and that it wasn't fair of him to just say no all the time. So he said that if I really wanted we could get married and that the more he thought about it the more he loved the idea, because nobody had ever loved him or trusted him enough to want to spend their life with him. And then he got down on one knee and he said that he was sorry he didn't have a ring, but I didn't mind that at all. I thought the fact that it was so spontaneous was romantic enough. And then I said yes. It just... it felt so right the way he asked me and everything else, and when I looked into his eyes I thought about all we had been through and even though not all of it has been good it's still a journey worth taking, and I really want to take this next step with him."

John listened thoughtfully and was certain that Melissa wasn't just saying this out of a desire to get married for marriage's sake. His features softened and now he finally did put his arms around her, hugging her tightly. Tears filled his eyes as he was overjoyed for her, and that was the moment when the emotion that she had been holding within herself came rushing through in a torrent.

"So what do you say?" she said moments afterwards when she was able to compose herself again, when she could dry her eyes. "Will you be my man of honor?"

"I'd love to," John said, "as long as Ryan doesn't mind. I know he's never had the highest opinion of me," he added, wearing a half smile.

Melissa dismissed his concern with a wave of the hand.

"That's all in the past. He doesn't have a problem with you at all. It was only at the beginning."

"Yeah, but it was pretty intense. Every time I saw him I thought he was going to rip my head off."

"Well, he thought you were a threat. I mean, I can see where he was coming from considering how close we are. Any guy would feel threatened. We share everything. It was funny though. I remember when he first told me about his concerns. He was so agitated I thought that something was really wrong, and then I finally asked him to tell me what was going through his mind and he made this big speech about how he didn't want to be a controlling guy and he didn't want to tell me who I could and couldn't be friends with, and that usually he wasn't jealous, but he just found it so hard to handle the fact that you're my best friend. It wasn't my proudest moment to burst out laughing when he revealed his fears, but it was so absurd to me. I think at first he didn't quite believe me when I told him you were gay. But he's over it now, I promise. It's been enough time."

"I know, I know, but it's not easy you know. I mean. I have heard a *lot* about your relationship. I just want to ask you one last time if you're sure that this is what you want because I've been there through all the tears and I've been there when you've ranted and raved and you've told me that you never want to see him again. I think it's a part of my man of honor duty to make sure that you're going into this with your eyes wide open."

This time Melissa didn't roll her eyes at him, nor did she react angrily. Instead she seemed grateful that he was taking the time to ask. "It's okay John. Like I said this is what I want. I know that my relationship hasn't always been perfect and there are moments when it could have gone the other way, but the fact that there's always been something that has brought us back together is significant. Either of us could have walked away a long time ago, but we didn't. We've both grown together, and I've seen him mature a lot as well. I want to see that continue. I want to see the kind of people that we can be together. I want to build a life with him, and he wants the same thing with me as well. At the end of the day I feel like we make each other better and that's the most important thing."

"Yes, I suppose it is," John said with a smile. "I'm really happy for you Melissa, and I can't wait for the wedding. It's going to be amazing. And I can't wait to be your man of honor either. I never thought it would actually happen."

"I told you when we were younger than I wanted you beside me when I got married."

"Yeah, but I thought that was just something you said. I thought that it was going to be the kind of thing that would fall by the wayside I mean, it's hardly normal, is it?"

"When have I ever cared about being normal?" Melissa said with a laugh upon her lips. John nodded along. It was one of the things he admired about her, this carefree attitude of hers, this feeling of adventure. It was something he lacked. His rational mind always struggled to take a leap without examining it from every angle, and perhaps that was why he was the one congratulating her on getting engaged rather than the other way around.

"So what's the next step now?" he asked.

"We're going to go shopping for a ring and then we're going to meet up and talk about the ceremony I think and what we exactly want from a wedding. I think the plan is to meet up with him and his best man for dinner."

"Sure, that sounds like it will be fun," John said. "Who is his best man?"

"Oh, this guy named Zee, I've never met him actually, but Ryan talks about him all the time."

"How can you have been together for so long and never met Ryan's best man?"

"Zee has been traveling the world for the past few years. He's a photographer, but he's home now apparently. They grew up together so they're pretty close."

"Wow… I bet he has a lot of stories to tell. Well, it'll be fun. I look forward to it."

"Me too," Melissa said. John basked in her glow. They spent the night toasting to happiness and talking about their future and their past. John's face ached from smiling so much, but in the back of his mind there were selfish thoughts as well, thoughts of envy with a bitter tang. He wondered if he would ever find someone he could share his life, he wondered if he would ever get to ask Melissa to be his best woman. There were certain things in life that only ever seemed to happen to certain people, and John feared he was always going to be the kind of man looking in on other people's happiness rather than experiencing his own. He didn't share any of this with Melissa of course, at least not yet. This was her night and she needed to be allowed to enjoy the good news.

Chapter Two

The bar was dark and grimy. Old rock music played on a jukebox. A group of guys were laughing around a pool table. Their gaze drifted away from the game whenever a woman walked by, and they leered. Zee brought the bottle of beer to his lips and enjoyed a slight smile. He had seen many things in many different parts of the world, but human nature was one of the constants. He'd only been back a few weeks, but it seemed as though the world had spun away from him. Everything had changed in his absence, or at least was in the process of changing. Zee had changed too, although sometimes he wondered if he was the only one that sensed it. When he returned home after his excursion around the world people acted as though he was the same as when he'd left. He wondered if they were blind to the change within him, or if he'd actually changed as much as he believed. When he had left he had been so shy and awkward, so unsure of himself, but throwing himself into the world had made him grow. It had brought him into this new awareness of himself and his body, and he would never be the same again.

He looked up as Ryan came in. Zee smiled at the appearance of his old friend. In truth there had been few things he missed from his old life, but the companionship of Ryan was one of them. Once upon a time he had thought he loved Ryan, but it had been a confusing time and over the course of a lot of soul searching he had come to learn that he had simply latched onto Ryan because Ryan had been the closest person to him. The feelings he had were intense, but they weren't romantic.

Zee rose from the table and clasped Ryan's hand. They embraced in a manly hug, pressing their chests against each other, before sitting down. Their initial reunion had come some time before, when Zee had first returned. Nothing seemed to have changed between them. They had picked up where they had left off, as though no time had passed at all. Of course there were so many things that had happened, including the fact that Ryan was in a long term relationship, something that Zee never thought would have happened.

"So I have some big news," Ryan said after he ordered a drink. "And I'm glad you're sitting down, because I think this might blow your mind. I'm getting married."

Zee had been in the middle of drinking when Ryan said this. He held the bottle to his lips, feeling the coolness of the round opening. Zee's eyes were beady. He had a husky look about him, for he had grown a thick dark beard over the course of his travels. His body was lean though, honed into a taut, sinewy form that any athlete would have been proud of. Ryan used to be the same, but the life of comfort had taken its toll and rounded his sharp edges.

"You're what?" Zee asked in disbelief.

"I'm getting married. I asked Melissa to marry."

"You did?"

"Will you stop reacting with a question," Ryan shot him a look. "Yes this is happening. Is it so hard to believe?"

"I mean given what I know about you..." Zee said, arching his eyebrows.

Ryan narrowed his eyes. "You've been gone for a long time. Things change."

"But this much? What happened to the guy who swore he was never going to get married, who wanted to live like Hugh Hefner? At school you could never get enough. Whenever anyone asked you to settle down you just laughed in their face. I remember a time when if a girl asked you to be serious that was the end of the relationship."

Ryan squirmed in his chair. "Yeah, well, that was a long time ago. I'm not proud of the way I used to be. I've grown. Melissa is special."

"She'd have to be to agree to marry your ass," Zee said with a laugh. "No man look, seriously, this is great news. I'm sorry that I didn't act like it was a big deal. I just never expected to hear those words coming from that mouth."

Ryan lifted his eyebrows and brought his drink to his lips. "To be honest I didn't either. When I went over there tonight I thought it was the end."

"What happened?"

"Well we got to talking and then things started to get heated and I remembered what you told me, about how I should just take a moment to breathe before I said anything and how I had to remember that it was the two of us against a situation rather than against each other. And I just listened to her tell me why it was important and I realized that I wanted to make her happy. She's changed me so much. The longer we've been together the more I've realized how fulfilling a relationship can be, and I'm not ready for it to end. It's not like she's sprung this on me before either. There was a time a few months into when we started dating where we had a conversation like this and it seemed as though we wanted different things. We could have ended it there, but neither of us wanted to, and I had the same feeling here as well. I don't want to be with anyone else, and if getting married is what I have to do to stay with her then that's what I'll do."

Zee looked thoughtful for a moment. "You know that you shouldn't feel as though this is something you *have* to do though, right? I mean, you shouldn't feel like you're being forced into anything."

"I'm not," Ryan reassured him. "It was more a figure of speech than anything else. What I meant to say is that I'm willing to consider other possibilities for my future than I was before."

"Well I'm glad, and I can't wait until I meet Melissa because I want to know what kind of woman could change you into this responsible, mature guy."

"Hey, a lot of it I did myself," Ryan said, although with the sense that he didn't quite believe it. Then the smile fell from his face and his tone dropped to something more serious. "Listen… I don't know how long you're sticking around for this time, but I'd really love it if you would be my best man. You know I'm not good at this emotional crap, but you know… we've been friends for a long time. You probably know me better than anyone else, and it would feel wrong having anyone else up there with me."

Zee was touched and it didn't take him any time to answer at all.

"Of course man. I'd love to. It would be my honor," he said.

Ryan sat there beaming. Then a moment of realization hit him. "

"Fuck," he said. "I'm getting married."

"Hell yeah you are," Zee said, and then promptly bought him a drink.

"So when am I going to get to meet her? I'm not going to have to wait until the wedding, am I?"

"Nah, I think we're going to go out for dinner, us two and Melissa and John."

"John?" Zee asked, arching an eyebrow at this unfamiliar name.

Ryan sighed a little and Zee got the impression that John wasn't his favorite person in the world. "He's her best friend. He's going to be her maid of honor, although they're calling it man of honor."

"That's interesting," Zee said.

"Yeah, I mean, he's gay so it's not like I have anything to worry about it's just... I don't know... it still just makes me feel weird, like something is wrong with her being so close to another guy."

"Have you spoke to her about it?"

"Oh yeah, a few times actually. She just says I'm being stupid. Like I said, he's gay so I don't have to worry about her running off with him or anything like that. It's just my own thing really. It took me a while to get used to it."

"What's he like?"

"He's a good guy, he's pretty quiet. But he had Melissa have been friends since they were kids. A little like us really. But yeah, it's just going to be a little twist to the usual wedding," he said.

"I'm sure it's going to be fine."

"Oh yeah. I don't think Melissa would have it any other way. Now, do I need to put you down as a plus one?"

Zee smiled. "I don't know about that," he said, letting a mocking laugh slip between his lips.

"Come on, I'm sure you could rustle up a date between now and then. I doubt it's that hard for you to find someone. I could probably put some feelers out if you wanted."

Zee shuddered. "The last thing I want is to be set up," he said. "Besides, I'm not really in that frame of mind right now. I'm still getting used to being back here. Maybe you can ask me again a little closer to the time," he said. Ryan shrugged and the conversation continued on, but Zee's mind was elsewhere, to a far corner of the world where he had left his heart. He bowed his head so that Ryan wouldn't see a crystal tear form in the corner of his eye.

Chapter Three

John wore the smartest shirt he could find as he wanted to treat this night as something special. Melissa had arranged for them all to meet at a restaurant simply called Bill's. The simple name belied its luxury and elegance. It was one of the brightest spots in the city, and John did not want to look out of place. His nerves fluttered as they always did when he was about to see Ryan. He knew he was being stupid for feeling this way considering he had known the man for a few years now, but they had never really connected in the way he had hoped. When he was younger he had often thought about what life was going to be like. He had assumed that once he and Melissa found boyfriends they would all be a happy group that went around like the Scooby gang, but it wasn't like that at all. Ryan was often curt around him, and they had only ever spent time together while around Melissa. Now there was going to be another guy, this Zee, and John was afraid that things were going to be like they were with Ryan.

He breathed deeply and told himself that there was no reason for that to be the case, and even that things might get better with Ryan now that he and Melissa were going to be married. John had to at least make the effort considering that Ryan was going to be around for a long time.

After Melissa had told him the news there were still moments when he couldn't actually believe it. It might have seemed cruel to some people, but if John were a betting man he would have doubled down on Melissa and Ryan breaking up. From what he knew of Ryan, the man just didn't seem the type to want to settle down. John wasn't about to say anything to Melissa, but he was still afraid that Ryan was going to change his mind or hurt her again. There had been too many tears shed already for this to be a flawless romance. Still, the fact that John had been chosen as man of honor was a great privilege and he was grateful to Melissa for acknowledging their close relationship, for he knew that Ryan couldn't have been enthused about it.

When he reached the restaurant evening had already set in. Candles were aflame, flickering and dancing on the tables, while string music played in the background. Shining cutlery gleamed in the light, set upon cream colored table clothes. The restaurant was filled with the murmuring of pleasant conversation. John saw a hand waving to him from the rear of the restaurant. Wine had already been poured and smiles were plastered on the faces of his three companions. Melissa rose from the table and gave him a warm hug. Ryan nodded and smiled, although John could see the tension on his face.

"I'm Zee, it's nice to meet you," Zee said, half rising from the table. He stretched out his arm and clasped John's hand. The touch was warm, leathery, strong.

"Nice to meet you too," John stammered out, for he was taken aback by Zee's presence. The man was trim, his head was bald, but it seemed as though it was by choice rather than by nature. A thick beard erupted from his chin and covered the lower half of his face, displaying his manliness. He wasn't a classically handsome man, the kind that would be on magazine covers or leading Hollywood films, but there was definitely something about him. He had a kind of aura, a presence that John found intoxicating. It was like the lure of the sun; you wanted to look, but knew that if you stared for too long you would get burned.

John took his seat and tried to stop his gaze darting toward Zee, as he didn't want the man to think of him as strange.

"Do you want to see what Ryan and I have been doing today?" Melissa asked, and promptly displayed her left hand, and the sparkling ring that sat upon her finger. It looked like it was the most expensive thing in the restaurant.

"Wow, that is beautiful," John said. "You have really good taste Ryan," he added, trying to make things run smoothly as he knew Melissa would appreciate it.

"Thanks, well, Melissa actually picked it out for herself. I thought I'd rather make sure she gets one she really likes than have to wear something just because I bought it for her," Ryan said.

"Well, it's lovely," John said, releasing Melissa's hand.

"It is. As soon as I saw it I knew it was the perfect one. I have the perfect ring and the perfect man, and I'm going to have the perfect wedding," she said, a beaming smile upon her face. She leaned in and shared a kiss with Ryan. John turned his eyes away as though he was witnessing something he shouldn't have. He shared a shy smile with Zee.

The waiter came over shortly and they ordered their food, while Ryan was excited to have another bottle of wine for the table. He seemed in good spirits and was more relaxed than John was used to. Melissa seemed happy as well, and that was the main thing.

"So have you thought about what kind of ceremony you want?" John asked while they waited for their meals to arrive.

"Well, we haven't really spoken about it yet. I mean, I figure we probably want the same thing, right?" Melissa said, looking toward Ryan.

"Probably, we tend to agree on a lot of things. I was thinking that we should have something a little different than normal. Too many people go for the traditional thing. We should be different, be really memorable, like maybe we could get married out on the water or something, or in the mountains. We could sort of set our love free in the world," Ryan spread his arm out as though he was reaching for the stars. John could tell from the look on Melissa's face that she was less than enthused. They had always spoken about what their dream weddings would be like, so when Ryan said that he didn't want anything traditional, John knew that it wasn't going to go down well.

"There is something to be said for traditional. It is a tradition for a reason after all," Melissa said diplomatically, trying to stress that it was something she was interested in, but Ryan was clearly glued to his idea of doing something different.

"People who want something traditional lack imagination. It's easy to do the same thing that everyone else is doing," he said. "We should try and be different, try and be really memorable."

"I don't know... I think there's something to be said for being traditional."

"You do?" Ryan asked, suddenly his voice went flat and all the excitement went out of his eyes.

Melissa nodded. "I do. It's what I've dreamed of since I was a little girl. I don't need the chapel or anything like that, but I'd like the white dress and the beautiful scenery and the sit down meal. It's classic and romantic for a reason," she said.

"Oh," Ryan said. "Well, I guess we have to talk about it a bit more than we might think. At least you don't want to get married in a chapel. I can't think of anything worse.

"Yeah, I guess we do have to think about what we both want." Melissa admitted. John caught her eye and hoped that this wasn't going to turn into a huge issue. Their food came, interrupting briefly, and then Ryan turned to Zee.

"You've seen plenty of different weddings around the world. What kind of things do you think would be cool for us?" he asked.

Zee's eyes widened, as though he realized he had been put on the spot. "Well, I mean, there are a lot of things people do. Traditional has a different meaning in every culture. I've seen people who get married in private and then have a huge party, I've seen people who have a huge party and hundreds of people are involved. I've seen people get married on the beach, I've seen people get married in the morning and then wait until the evening before they properly celebrate, having a period in between to reflect on what it means and how they're going to progress through life. I've also known people who have gone into the wilderness away from everything else in the world to be with the one person they adore most of all and they say their vows in front of nature. The one thing that I've learned about all of them is that there's always something special about it, because it's about the person you're marrying not the things surrounding you."

"That's really lovely Zee. I can't wait to hear your best man speech," Melissa said. John nodded in agreement. He was touched by the gentle emotion in Zee's voice, and even more intrigued about the life this man had lived and the things that he had experienced.

"I like the idea of getting married in the middle of nowhere, just as and the world. What more do we need?" Ryan said, the excited gleam returning to his eyes.

"That's not going to happen," Melissa said sharply. "You know that one of the reasons I want to get married is because my grandparents aren't going to be around forever. I'd feel awful if I got married and they couldn't be there," she said. Ryan frowned and sighed a little, poking his meat with his fork.

"I mean we shouldn't have to feel obliged to invite people. It's our day after all."

"But it's not Ryan. A wedding isn't just about the two people getting married, it's also about all the friends and family who attend. It's about sharing and celebrating together. I know a lot of people elope, but it's not something I could ever imagine doing."

"I think it sounds a lot more peaceful to me. There's less chance for anything to go wrong, less chance for drama."

"What do you mean?" Melissa asked. John detected the edge to her voice. He wasn't sure if Ryan did too. Ryan's senses seemed to have been dulled by the wine; he'd had more of it than anyone else at the table.

"I just mean that the more people involved, the more chance there is for something to go wrong. I just don't want there to be something crazy that happens that takes the sheen away from us."

"And you think my grandparents are going to do that?"

"No, not them I just... I don't know... all that matters to me is that you're there. As long as you're there then I'm happy. I don't need the big occasion. I just want to be there and say that I love you and promise myself to you. The fact that other people are there is completely incidental to me."

Melissa stared at him. "So you don't care about family or anything else?" she asked.

Ryan let out a choking laugh. "Melissa, I don't really care about the wedding that much. All I care about is being with you."

John visibly winced when Ryan said that. It was a difficult thing to watch a man shoot himself. Melissa's entire demeanor changed. Her voice was ice and she rose in one swift movement.

"I need to get some air," she said, and she was gone in an instant. Ryan sat there eating his dinner, shaking his head.

"Women," he said, rolling his eyes. Then he caught himself. "I guess you two wouldn't know about that."

John glanced across the table at Zee to see if Zee was thinking the same thing he was.

"I think you should go and talk to her man," Zee said.

"What? Why? She just needs to let off a little steam. She gets like this sometimes, you know, emotions run high and stuff. You know it, right John?" he asked, nodding in John's direction.

Despite this being the perfect opportunity to form a bond with Ryan, John wasn't willing to betray Melissa to do so.

"I think this time she might have a reason," he said.

"What do you mean?" Ryan asked.

"You just said that you don't care about the wedding," Zee said, dumbfounded.

"Yeah, I don't. What I care about is marrying her. That's the most important thing. I don't see what's so wrong about that. Other people come and go you know, and the wedding doesn't mean a thing if she's not there," Ryan said. "I don't know what's so bad about that."

"I think it's the way you said it. You should go and talk to her. Just because the wedding isn't that important to you, doesn't mean it's the same for her. She needs to know that you're invested in this as much as her and that you're not just along for the ride," Zee said.

Ryan chewed on the food in his mouth and then rolled his eyes. He dabbed a napkin against the corners of his mouth and then rose from the table, muttering to himself as he left in pursuit of Melissa, leaving John and Zee alone.

"Trouble in paradise already," John remarked with a slight twitch of the lips. Zee arched his eyebrows.

"He's never really been the tactful sort."

"No, he hasn't. You've only just come back from a trip around the world, right, has he told you about all the troubles they've had?" John asked.

"Not in great detail. He told me that they've come close to breaking up a few times, but he didn't say why."

"Well, a lot of times its miscommunication. Sometimes I think Ryan never learned how to talk to people."

"He wasn't given many good role models. His Dad left when he was a kid, and then his Mom worked all the time. He was around my place more often than not, but as much as we tried to make him a part of our family there's only so far we could go. He just didn't get the same attention as most kids do."

"I had no idea," John said, and suddenly felt guilty for thinking the worst of Ryan. Sometimes it was difficult to remember that everyone had a reason for being the way they were.

"Still, he should have learned better by now. I can't believe he actually said he doesn't care about the wedding. What a rookie mistake," Zee shook his head and laughed in disbelief. It helped to break the tension. John had never been that good with strangers, but there was something different about Zee.

"So what were you doing out in the world? Melissa mentioned that you're a photographer?" John asked.

"Yeah," Zee replied, leaning back in his seat. He poured a little more wine in his glass and offered some to John, but John refused. He didn't want to risk any verbal slip ups of his own. "I worked for a nature magazine, but I'm home now."

"It must have been amazing to see all those different places. What made you come home?"

Zee shrugged. "You know, there comes a point where you travel so much that you start to lose yourself, you know, you meet all these people but then you move on and you have to do the same thing all over again. I guess I started to wonder if these people really knew me at all. There's something liberating about being able to be anyone, but then you start questioning yourself. I just wanted to come home and rediscover who I am really, come back to people who knew me before I left."

"You think you'll stay for a while or are you planning to head back out there? I imagine you must be the kind of person who gets itchy feet.

"I used to, but I'm not sure. When I first left here I couldn't wait to get away but now... I don't know. I'm just taking some time to figure out what I'm doing. I'm going to work on a collection of photos, which will be nice to take a break from nature, and then we'll see what happens. I'm not really too concerned about the future. I'll just take it as it comes. I'm going to be around for a while at least," he added, nodding to the empty chairs.

"I wish I had your attitude. I don't think I could ever be that laid back," John admitted.

Zee smiled. "I never used to be. I used to think that I had to be a certain way, or that things had to turn out in a particular manner, but then I learned that life takes its twists and turns and at the end of the day all you can do is do something that makes you happy."

"What happened to change your mind like that?"

Zee played with his food. "I was supposed to go to college. It was a big deal to my family. There had never been anyone in my family go to college before and they wanted me to be the first. I was never a genius or anything, but I did all right for myself, but then I just didn't make it. My parents had saved up so much money for a college fund and they had wanted it so badly for me that it almost seemed like it *had* to happen, but it just didn't. It was as though everything my life had been building toward just didn't matter any longer, and I wasn't sure what to do with myself. My parents were angry. I didn't know if they were angrier at me, themselves, the colleges, or just the world in general. I could tell they thought I was a failure, but I didn't want to define myself by whether I got into college or not. To be honest I'd never liked the whole academic grind anyway. I preferred to just do my own thing, so I started taking photographs and submitted a few to some magazines. Ended up getting a contract with one of them and I never looked back."

"Wow, that is really incredible. I can't believe that I'm sitting with someone who did that. It's just... I really wish I had that sense of adventure."

"It's not always as easy or exciting as you'd think," Zee said, but his modesty only made it all the more impressive.

"This might sound like a stupid question, but is there one place in the world you like above everywhere else? Do you have a favorite place?" John asked. He didn't care that it was the kind of question Zee had probably been asked a thousand times.

Zee blew out his cheeks and arched his eyebrows as he thought. "I don't know. There are loads of places that I liked for different reasons. I suppose that there was one time I was sailing down this river in a ravine. The walls of nature stretched out high above me and the way the sun set, well, it looked as though the sky was bleeding. I just remember thinking to myself that this moment is never going to come again, and I was the only one witnessing something so beautiful. I was there, present in the world, and it was just this really serene, perfect moment. At the time it seemed like it was going to last forever, but I suppose nothing ever does."

There was a tinge of sorrow as he spoke those last few words, but John's heart was touched by the emotion in Zee's voice. There was a beauty and eloquence to them that drew him in like a moth to a flame. It was rare that someone should spark something within him so suddenly, and all he wanted was to listen to Zee speak more about his travels and all he had experienced. But just as another question was upon John's lips, Ryan and Melissa returned. They seemed calmer, although it was clear to John that Melissa had been crying. Ryan wore an awkward smile and John vowed to himself that if Ryan hurt Melissa, he would pay. The conversation turned back to the wedding and John had to table his intrigued feelings about Zee for now, but he definitely wanted to hear more, and he was already thinking about an excuse to see the man again.

Chapter Four

It had been a long night for Zee, and one that almost ended in disaster for Ryan. At least he and Melissa had come back to the table and seemed to be on an even keel again. Ryan hadn't changed as much as Zee had believed. He still had an uncanny knack for putting his foot in his mouth. John seemed nice though, although Zee hadn't been prepared to talk about his traveling experiences with a stranger. He surprised himself with how honest he was, although he had kept some things back. There were some matters that other people simply didn't need to know about. It struck him as funny how people were so amazed at him for traveling around the world when it had always been second nature to him. There were definitely moments when he appreciated the world he was seeing, but there were other times when it didn't seem that special at all. A place was just a place and people were just people. They were dotted all over the world and were unending in their constancy. It was rare to find a place that was untouched by humanity's gaze. In some ways it struck him as a shame that this would be the case, that humans had spread their web so vast there was no place to escape, but in another sense it was reassuring. It meant that no matter where anyone went there would always be the chance of seeing someone to help. It meant that nobody would ever have to be alone.

Alone... the word weighed heavily on Zee's mind. Sorrow filled his heart as he thought about the past and all he had left behind. He knew he would never be able to get it back.

His Mom, Anita, was still awake when he returned.

"Did you have a nice time?" she asked. It pained him to look at her. He remembered her as being such a vibrant woman, so filled with energy and life. When he returned he realized that she was little more than a shadow of her former self, and he felt guilty because he knew his absence had played some part in this. Her hair had lost its dark luster, and perennial sadness lingered in her eyes. The house seemed quiet as well. On the walls hung pictures he had taken that had been displayed in magazines, small pieces of his life over the last few years. There were other pictures too, ones that elicited more emotion, such as the ones of his father. The void left by him was palpable.

"I did. Ryan's fiancée seems lovely."

"I'm so happy for him," Anita said. "It's such a joy to know that he's settling down. He always was such a troubled young man. I'm glad that he's found his path in life."

"Yeah."

"It gives hope for us all," she said.

A lump appeared in his throat.

"I'm not sure that kind of life is really for me," he said, hating himself for saying it because he knew it would have meant the world to her. He wanted to tell her how sorry he was for not being the son she wanted him to be, for not being able to give her what she wanted.

"You know too many people go through this life alone. You can't always pretend that you're an island Zee. You deserve to be happy."

"I am happy Mom," he said, "I promise. It's just been a long night and I'm pretty tired. I'm still getting used to being back here."

"I know. I'm glad that you're going to be sticking around for a little while. I've missed you. We both did."

"I know," Zee said, and bowed his head so that he didn't have to look at her. He was at home, but he hadn't come back quickly enough. He hadn't come back to say goodbye to his father.

"I missed you too," he added, before the pause was too long. Anita walked up to him and squeezed his arm. Maybe she knew that he was lying.

"I know things haven't been easy, but this will always be your home. You can stay here for as long as you like. It's just a shame that he's not here to enjoy your company as well."

Zee smiled wryly. "I think the place would be a lot noisier. He'd always be yelling at me to do this or that, and he'd probably still be telling me that I should get a proper job rather than be a photographer."

Anita smiled. "Yes, he probably would have. He was proud of you though. I hope you know that. Whenever everyone came round he always showed off your pictures and told them that you took them, and he always got more than one copy of the magazine to show people. I know the two of you didn't always get on, but he was proud of you."

Zee nodded. Emotion welled up inside him and he found that his insides churned. Tears filled his eyes. He had been so used to bottling it all up inside him in his solitude that he wasn't sure how to express it to anyone else. He mumbled a goodnight to his mother and then ventured upstairs to his room. He had enough money to afford a place of his own, but until he figured out what he wanted to do he decided he was going to stay here. It felt good to be at home anyway, and the presence of his mother was reassuring. After being on his own for so long there was something comforting about being back in the bosom of his parent. It was just a shame that only his mother had been waiting for him.

Zee shut the door to his room and enjoyed the quiet darkness. He switched on a lamp and the dull glow illuminated the room and made shadows long on the wall. He opened a draw and pulled out a box in which he had kept mementos of his trip. There was one in particular that meant a lot to him, a photograph that had been folded and bent and dog eared, but it still brought a smile to his face. Behind him was a long river, and the sky bled red. He had lied to John earlier that night because he hadn't been alone in that perfect moment. Instead he had been with a man he had loved, a man who was now a part of his past, yet Zee wasn't able to let him go, not completely, not even though he was half a world away.

Warm tears trickled down his cheeks and his shoulders shuddered, hidden from the world.

***

Zee received a surprising message a few days later. It was from John, inviting him out for a drink to talk about best man and man of honor things. Zee's first inclination was to decline the invitation as he didn't particularly want to spend time with new people, but he knew that wasn't any way to live, and as best man he did have responsibilities, so he accepted.

They met at a small bar along a strip in the middle of the city. There were clubs that were opening their doors, and already scantily clad women and hunter men were going inside, ready to relinquish their inhibitions and give into their primal instincts while pounding music thundered inside their minds. Zee turned away and entered the small bar where he was meeting John. John was already there. He smiled and waved, and Zee walked up to him. John had a nervous energy about him. He had already torn the label off his beer, and his gaze darted about furtively.

"I'm glad you agreed to meet tonight. I thought it would be a good idea for us to go over a few things and make sure that we're on the same page. I think if this wedding is going to go smoothly we're going to have to work together," John said, although Zee wasn't sure if that was the entire reason why John had asked him. There was a definite kind of energy between the two of them, and it almost frightened Zee because it was too easy to talk to John.

"Sure thing, especially if Ryan is going to put his foot in his mouth over and over again."

"I know. I have to keep reminding Melissa that he doesn't necessarily mean everything he's saying. It's hard to cope with though, especially when he does it so often," John said.

"Yeah, I guess it must be hard for him though. He never had a serious relationship before Melissa."

"I suppose I shouldn't be too surprised. They almost ended before they had even begun."

"Because he was jealous of you?"

"He told you about that, did he?" John said.

"He mentioned it. But he's over it now."

"That's a relief. I still get the sense that he doesn't like me."

"I don't think it's that at all. Ryan has always been the territorial type. I think he's just unsure about how to handle certain things because as I said before he was never taught how. I'm pretty sure that he's just worried because he knows that you and Melissa have a kind of bond that he can never touch on. You grew up together, right?"

"Yeah, but he knows he doesn't have anything to worry about. I don't know if he told you, but I'm gay."

"He did. I'm gay as well," Zee said.

John nodded. There was a moment of silence between the two of them. They understood that they shared something profound, something that not everyone could comprehend.

"What was it like for you?" John asked. The question wasn't specific, but it didn't need to be. Zee knew exactly what he meant.

"It was hard at times, confusing. Sometimes I didn't know where I fit in or where I was going to belong."

"What did your parents think about it?"

"They were supportive actually. They were the first ones I told. I thought they were going to be angry, especially Dad, but in the end they just wanted me to be happy. I think a part of them was upset that they weren't going to be able to enjoy a wedding or a grandchild, but they recognized that it was my own life to live and they never tried to make me feel bad for it."

John nodded. "Melissa was the first person I told. It's not that I didn't trust my parents or anything, it was just that we shared everything with each other. She laughed and said that she knew because she had caught me looking at some of the other guys at school. I guess we've always known each other better than we've known ourselves. It's part of why we're such good friends. She was really understanding. And then when I came out to my parents she was there with me."

Zee was surprised at this. "You two really are close."

John nodded and smiled widely. "We really are. Well, you and Ryan are as well. How did he react when you told him?"

Zee laughed and leaned back in his chair, shaking his head slightly.   "Man that is a long time ago. I wish I could say it went the same way, but things were different. Like I said, Ryan hasn't always been the best at handling his emotions. He was confused at first. To be honest I just don't think he liked the fact that things were changing. We spoke about it a lot and he just didn't seem to understand why I wouldn't like girls," Zee laughed as he said this, "but eventually he managed to come through for me and things were the same as they ever were. Then a while later I left anyway, so it wasn't like he needed to be awkward around me."

"Well I'm glad he managed to grow out of that. Did he keep in touch with you when you were on your travels?"

"I sent letters here and there, mostly just to Mom and Dad, but I told them to pass along messages to my friends. I had email of course, whenever I could get to a computer."

"I bet they're glad to have you home. Are things awkward between you? Have they gotten over the fact that you didn't go to college?" John asked.

Zee's tone dropped. "Actually my Dad is dead. That's another reason why I came back. I had to learn it in an email. I knew I had to come back straight away. I guess I always figured that they were going to be waiting for me when I came back but then... well... it didn't turn out to be that way."

"I'm sorry to hear that," John said. The mood dropped as it did whenever anyone mentioned death, as though grief was a shared thing even among people who didn't know the deceased. Zee was tired of everything he touched sinking into melancholy though.

"But we're not here to talk about that. We're supposed to talk about the wedding," Zee said. John nodded and although it was a little awkward at first they managed to break through the gloom and move onto a happier subject.

"So I don't know if this is normal because I've never been in this position before, but I think we need to talk about what's going to happen, especially after the other night. I know Melissa was polite about it, but I know that she has some strong ideas for the wedding and if she and Ryan don't come together to have something they both want it's going to be a disaster."

"So she's set on something traditional?" Zee asked.

John nodded. "And she has been since we were kids. She's always been the kind of bride to want to have the white dress and the red roses. It might seem simple and plain to other people, but all Melissa has wanted is to give her family a good memory and to have something that lasts. I get that Ryan wants to put his own spin on things and I'm by no means saying that this is just something for Melissa, but there's no way that she's going to want to do anything out of the ordinary."

Zee nodded. "When I wasn't shooting for the magazine I did some work as a wedding photographer now and then, so I've seen what happens when the bride and groom aren't on the same page. It's never good. I'll try and bring him around."

"And I'll try and find out what new and exciting things Melissa is open to," John said. "I just couldn't believe it when he said that he didn't care about the wedding."

"That's Ryan for you. There's never been a situation he couldn't make worse by putting his foot in his mouth," Zee said with a laugh. "He doesn't mean it really. Like I said, he's matured a lot from when I knew him before."

"Yeah. I can't say the same about Melissa. She's always had a good head on her shoulders and she always knows the right thing to do. I know that he's your friend, so I hope that you don't take offence at this, but I have always been a little surprised about how much Melissa has been willing to put into this relationship. I mean, I guess I always thought that she'd end up with someone who was just as sensible as her."

"I guess there's something to be said for opposites attracting," Zee said. "But deep down Ryan is a good guy. He won't treat her badly. He knows better than that, sometimes he just doesn't know when to shut his mouth," Zee laughed.

They drank more and learned a little more about each other. Zee was happy to let John do the talking. His words became a little hazier the more he drank, a little more slurred. Zee was just glad for a while to have the focus off of him and his experiences. It seemed to be all anyone wanted to talk about when he came back. At least the wedding would do well to take people's attention away from him. Sometimes it was easier to forget about what happened before, to try and push it away rather than embrace it because it was too hard. If he hadn't gone away then he would have been able to say goodbye to his father. If he had stayed then he wouldn't be the same man he was now. It was a difficult conundrum and there wasn't anything he could do about it now, but the pain still stung and he wished more than anything that it could go away.

He wore a false smile for the rest of the evening. John didn't seem to notice. It reminded Zee of when he was out traveling, how he would meet someone random and share a conversation, get a glimpse of someone else's life. But this time was different. This time he wasn't going to be moving on.

Chapter Five

"You're late," Melissa said as John staggered up to the café. He wore sunglasses, which helped to dull the ache from the glaring sun, but it did nothing to stem the throbbing headache inside. The world seemed to lurch around him whenever he moved, and he was glad of the respite that greeted him when he sank into the chair.

"I know. I'm sorry. It was a big night," he said quietly, and ordered some coffee. A motorbike sputtered and roared across the road, taking off at an extreme speed. John winced and glared in that direction, the loud noise echoed in his mind.

Melissa smirked. "I never thought you'd turn out to be a party animal," she said.

"I'm not. It's just that one drink turned into another and... well... I guess it's the oldest story in the book," John groaned.

"I take it Zee is good company?"

"He is. Really good guy. Ryan made a good choice. Sad story as well."

"Yeah, Ryan mentioned that he's been through a lot. It must have been so sad for him to be away when his father died. I couldn't imagine that. It's one of the things that has always made me wary about going away. I've never been able to think about what I might miss out on at home, or what bad news might come to haunt me. It's good that he was able to come back though. There's nothing like being at peace with family," she said.

John nodded.

"So what did you talk about?" she asked.

"Oh, just stuff," John said. "Mostly about the wedding." They had also spoken a lot about his own life as well. He had intended to ask Zee more about his experiences out in the world, but Zee had had the uncanny ability to shift the conversation onto John's life, as unremarkable as it was in comparison.

"Well I hope you two aren't going to meddle. This is still mine and Ryan's day," Melissa said with an arched eyebrow.

"Don't worry, we're not going to meddle. We just want to make sure the day runs smoothly."

"Good. I am sorry about the way I reacted at dinner. I didn't think it would get to me so much, what Ryan said I mean."

"Well you were within your rights to act like that. He doesn't always know the right thing to say."

"Yeah, but I should have given him the benefit of the doubt I just... I guess I'm just afraid."

"Of what?"

Melissa gnawed on her lower lip and drummed her nails on the table. "You're going to think I'm stupid."

"When has that ever stopped you from telling me something before?" John asked. Melissa shot him a snide look.

"I just worry that something is going to happen to my grandparents before the wedding, like they've waited so long for this to come and something is going to stop them. I love Ryan, I just want this all to go off without a hitch and that's why I want to keep it simple. The more complicated we try and make it or the more adventurous we try and make it, the more chance there is for something to go wrong."

"I understand where you're coming from, but you have to remember that this is Ryan's wedding too," John said patiently. "And you shouldn't let yourself be ruled by fear. Besides, isn't one of the reasons you're with Ryan because he pushes you out of your comfort zone and gets you to embrace new aspects of life?"

Melissa sighed and nodded. "You're right. I just don't want it turning into anything tacky or cheap. I don't want my wedding to be a carnival."

"I'm sure it won't be," John said reassuringly. "Ryan wouldn't have asked you to marry him if he didn't want to get married, and he definitely doesn't want you to be unhappy. It's all going to be fine and your grandparents are going to be so proud to walk you down the aisle. And you've already made sure that things have such little chance to go wrong because you want the wedding as soon as possible."

"Yeah, which means we have a lot to get on with. I have to pick out my dress, we have to sort out the florist and the cake, and then there's the matter of the food and the seating plan and the actual venue and the honeymoon and…"

John reached out to place his hand upon hers, hoping to steady her frantic voice. "We'll just take it one step at a time and tick things off as they come. There's plenty of time for us to get this done and it's all going to be perfect," he said. Melissa breathed a little easier after this and John was glad that he could help her relax. He wondered if she was going to be this bad on the day itself, but he was determined to enjoy living vicariously through her as he didn't think he would get to experience this for himself. It gave the whole endeavor a sad tint, but he wasn't going to let that show to Melissa.

They spent the morning making a list of everything they needed to do in preparation for the wedding, and it was one hell of a list. They next divided it into tasks between her and Ryan to help split the load, although John made a mental note to speak with Zee to make sure that Ryan didn't get too crazy with his ideas. By the time he and Melissa were done they had an organized plan and Melissa was feeling better about the whole thing. Now as long as everything followed the plan it would all be all right. But there was something that John couldn't count on, and that was for Melissa to have more on her mind than the wedding.

"So... is there any chance of anything happening between you and Zee?" she asked.

John acted as though the very notion of it took him by surprise.

"Why would you even say anything like that?" he asked.

Melissa narrowed her eyes. "Don't play coy with my John. I know when you're interested in someone. It hasn't escaped my attention that you've been itching to spend time with him."

"I'm just doing my man of honor duty. I wouldn't want the wedding to be a disaster because of a lack of communication," John said defensively.

"Why even try lying to me John? You know it's not going to work. I know all your secrets," she said.

John sighed and knew that it was indeed hopeless. He shrugged and let his defenses down.

"Fine, you've got me. Yes I may have a little bit of a crush on Zee, and I may have used my position as man of honor to engineer a situation in which we might spend more time together just in case there is anything there."

"I have no problem with this," Melissa said. "Zee seems like a great guy and you know I've been wanting you to find someone special for too long now. But I hope that this is going to be something serious. I don't want you to have some kind of a fling and then it all blows up in your face and suddenly the wedding is awkward because the best man and the man of honor can't bear to face each other."

John wore a thin smile. "You know I'd never do that to you," he said. "Besides, I don't know if anything is actually going to happen."

"You don't think he's into you?"

John sighed. "In all honesty I'm not sure. We had a great time together, but I feel like he's holding back about something. Maybe it's just me seeing something that's not there. He's not like any other guy I've ever known," he said.

"He has certainly led an interesting life," Melissa agreed. "I think you should just tell him how you feel."

John's mouth dropped open, aghast. "I can't do that!" he gasped.

"Why not? We're not in high school anymore John. We don't have to play these games. We're adults. Just tell him that you like him and you want to go out on a date. What's the worst that can happen?"

"I don't know, he could laugh in my face and then everyone else around us would start laughing too and then I'd be a joke, as though the very idea of anyone dating me is so absurd that nobody could take it seriously."

Melissa gave him a sympathetic look. "I know that was a painful memory, but it was a long time ago and just because it happened once it doesn't mean it's going to happen again. Besides, I don't think Zee is like Lenny. History isn't going to repeat itself, I promise. The thing is John that if you don't take a risk now and then nothing exciting is ever going to happen. That's what happened with Ryan and me. He didn't think I would be interested in him, but then he asked me and I gave it a shot and look us now, we're getting married! Good things can happen if you give things a chance," she said.

John nodded. He knew she was right. It was a clear and obvious truth that he could not deny with any sense of rationality, but the very thought of it was enough to make him shudder. Taking risks had never come naturally to him. He was the type to stay in the shadows and play it safe, but then again he was tired of seeing other people get the glory. Maybe it was time for him to finally shed the trappings of his own mind and let Zee know how he felt.

***

Nothing John did ever came quickly, so a couple of weeks elapsed as he tried to work up the courage to tell Zee how he really felt. Melissa kept nagging him and telling him to buck his ideas up, but it never came easily to him. However, he was tired of always living in a world of what if and what might have been, and he was certain that a man like Zee wouldn't be single forever. John had seen too many other men come and go, and he was tired of suffering the same old heartbreak.

He and Zee had still been spending time together, and the more time they spent together the more John saw him as someone special. He had a unique way of looking at the world, and John had also looked up some of the pictures Zee had taken. They were breathtaking. It amazed him how someone could have been able to capture so much beauty of the world in a single frame. His pictures were like art. There was something about them that came alive. It gave John a thrill to think that he knew the man behind the camera, the man that had preserved these moments for eternity.

They had mostly worked on the wedding together and discussed how they could help Melissa and Ryan with the various tasks that needed to be done, and occasionally a few personal things slipped in, but for the most part they spoke about the wedding. John was a little surprised at this as he thought he would be able to break through Zee's outer shell and get to the personal stuff, but aside from that initial night where Zee had spoken about some things that bothered him, Zee had mostly been quiet and reticent to speak about his true feelings.

However, after they had finished up on this particular night, John was determined to not let the opportunity slip away. They were sitting on a sloping park, high up where they could see the sea stretching out to the edge of the world. Folders and bits of paper were scattered around them. The air was calm, so no breeze threatened to carry them away. Fluffy clouds drifted lazily through the sky and around them there were clusters of people. Some were walking their dogs, others were couples lost in each other, while some families played with their kids. Frisbees soared through the air and the happy laughter was a pleasant addition to the local ambience.

"So how does this compare to the rest of the world?" John asked.

Zee let out a dry chuckle. "It has its own charm. Honestly? Every place has something about it, but I guess since it's my home it does mean a little more to me than other places. Maybe memories of a place make it a little more beautiful," he said, but he didn't elaborate further.

"You don't talk about your trip around the world as much as I thought you would have."

"What do you mean?"

John shrugged. "Most people when they go traveling can't shut up about it when they come back. I know a guy who went to England when he was a kid and he still mentions it now whenever England is mentioned."

"Yeah, I never wanted to be like that. I went out there to do a job and I don't know... sometimes I think sharing memories makes them more special, and sometimes I think keeping them private does the same thing. It's a thin line to straddle."

John nodded, pretending that he understood. "I looked up some of your work. It's really good."

"Thank you," Zee said sincerely.

"I just can't imagine what it's like to see so many cultures. You must have learned so much, both about yourself and about the world around you. I don't think I could be as tight lipped as you are. I think I'd be telling everyone all the time," John said.

Zee smiled. "Maybe I will in time. I guess I'm still getting used to being back home. It's almost like when I was away I was a different person. People back here have memories of me from before I left. In a way I'm relearning what it is to be myself as well."

"I never knew you before you left."

"I know. Maybe that's why I find it easy to talk to you."

"I'm glad. I could use another friend, especially since things with Melissa are going to change when she gets married."

"Yeah, I guess the same is true of Ryan as well. Marriage changes a lot of things. Especially if they have a kid."

"Yeah," John nodded. He hadn't really spent much time thinking about what the future was going to be like. His friendship with Melissa had always been a huge part of his life, but soon it was just going to be a smaller part of hers and he couldn't expect her to devote as much time to him as she used to.

"That is one thing I learned actually," Zee said, "is that things always change and it's really the only thing that we can count on in the world. Sometimes it was tough to leave places behind, but just because something ended it didn't mean my life was over. It's still hard though sometimes, to leave things behind, to think about what might have been."

"Do you have any regrets?" John asked.

Zee took a moment to respond, and then slowly shook his head, but he didn't say what those regrets were.

"To be honest I've lived my life with regrets. I always wanted to make sure that I didn't make a mistake, so I never bothered to do anything unless I was sure that it was going to succeed. I wouldn't like to count how many times I missed out on something special because I wasn't willing to go that extra mile." He looked at Zee, wishing that Zee would pick up on what he was trying to say because it would make things easier. But things never happened that way.

John saw this as a test. He trembled with nerves and had to quell the wild emotion that surged within him. A lump formed in his throat and when he spoke next the words felt as heavy as lead, and they acted as though they didn't want to escape from the confines of his mouth.

"Zee... there's something I want to tell you. I'm not really sure... I mean... in the past I've always played it safe, but I'm tired of doing that. One of the things that I like about you is that you have an adventurous spirit. I guess it's one of the things that first caught my attention. And I know this might be a little bit awkward because we're both involved in the wedding, but I also don't want to keep silent and end up regretting it like I have done in the past. So I guess, well, what I'm trying to say is that I'd like to get to know you better and spend more time together and just... you know... make things a bit more special."

John cringed at himself for stammering and spluttering. It was as though all his practice at speaking during the course of his life counted for nothing. Halfway through his little speech he could feel himself faltering and regretted ever having started, but he the momentum carried him to the end, and then he just wanted the ground to swallow him up as he had convinced himself that Zee wasn't going to be interested. He averted his gaze, but he supposed it was better that the sentiment had been expressed, and it was better that it had been done now so they still had time before the wedding to get over the awkwardness.

Zee didn't say anything in return. At first John thought this was confirmation of his worst fears and all the horrible moments of the past came rushing through his mind in a torrent of shame. This was just another one to add to the list, he lamented, another moment that would always torture him and make him more nervous the next time he found a man who captured his attention. But then he felt something brushing a hand. He looked up and saw Zee smiling at him.

"That's really sweet," Zee said. John's breath caught in his throat. He thought Zee was going to say more, but as it turned out no more needed to be said. John leaned in. With the touch of Zee's hand upon his, John felt emboldened to take another risk, and it was most definitely a risk worth taking. The world melted away. The sounds of the other people in the park faded into the distance, secondary to the song that rang out inside John's mind. He closed his eyes and felt the warm, sweet breath upon his lips before their mouths crashed together in a tender kiss. It had been so long since John had felt anything like this he almost felt as though he was dreaming, but the sensations were so powerful, so real, so intoxicating he knew it couldn't be anything but real. Zee was there, clear and present before him, inhabiting his entire world. John's mind was alive with the scent and touch of the man, with the taste of him, and he wanted more. When they broke apart they were both smiling. John's eyes sparkled with delight and it felt as though a new world had opened up to him. Melissa had been right. A risk had been worth taking, but what came next?

John wasn't sure, but he was just glad that Zee had responded in a pleasant way. Zee was indeed a man of mystery though, and John wished that he knew what was going on behind the man's eyes. He supposed there was time for all of that to be learned though. For now he just had to enjoy being in the thrall of this excitement.

⁂

They walked away from the park. Each of them were holding the folders and paperwork, which disappointed John as he wanted to hold Zee's hand. When John offered Zee a lift home, Zee accepted. When they reached Zee's house, John realized that he wasn't ready to part just yet.

"I don't know if this is too presumptuous of me or not," John said, "but are there any more photos you can show me? Maybe some more that aren't in the magazines?" It was a weak pretense, and he was certain that Zee would be able to see through it, but John didn't particularly care, especially not when Zee nodded. He explained that he lived with his Mom for the time being, although she seemed to be out when they entered. Zee led John up to his room and pulled open a folder filled with photos. Each one was more beautiful than the last and once again John was overwhelmed with pride and excitement that he should know the man responsible for taking these.

"They're so beautiful," he said. Zee sat beside him. The mattress creaked a little under their weight. Zee's presence filled the room. John loved feeling the energy that emanated from him. John looked up and was struck by the look in Zee's eyes. It was something profound and deep, filled with emotion. John only wished that he knew what was going on behind those eyes.

"Talk to me Zee. Tell me what you're thinking," he said softly, but it didn't seem as though Zee was in the mood for talking. He took the folder away from John's lap and flung it on the floor before leaping on John. John yelped a little, taken aback by the sudden passionate lunge. Zee's arms curled around him, running through his hair and down his back, while lips

51

crashing against his mouth. John sank into the bed. The softness of the pillow contrasted with the hardness and the heat of Zee's body, of his intent. John felt a knot twisting inside him. There had been so many lonely nights, so many times when his flesh had been left unscorched by the touch of another man, but here was Zee with his ardent fingers that were tearing everything away, here was Zee with his lust and his energy and everything that John could ever want.

John surrendered inside, kissing back with equal ardor. He ran his hands up and down Zee's back, feeling the surprisingly lean and tight muscles. Zee's beard was soft and tickled John, while the sensations were wild and unfamiliar, so much so that John felt as though feathers were teasing him. He closed his eyes and surrendered to the passion. In one moment he wondered what he was going to tell Melissa about all this, in another Melissa was the farthest thing from his mind as there was only the blistering passion. Zee was filled with this animalistic, savage intensity. It was raw and hot and John had never been wanted this severely before. It was as though Zee craved him, and John was happy to be his prey.

Eventually there was a break from the kissing. John gasped for breath. His skin was flushed and his body was crying out for more. Everything was hard and rigid, and he had felt all of Zee's hardness as well, albeit through clothes. It was a promise of more, an intention that was beckoning with its lust and John whimpered when Zee left the bed, whispering that he just needed to go to the bathroom.

John was aching to get out of his clothes. They were like a prison. He could feel the swollen desire and he had to blink because he saw stars. God it had been so long, but Zee would soon set him right. John wanted to get ready. He looked around to see where Zee might keep his condoms. Although John had been prepared to take a risk to tell Zee how he felt, he hadn't expected things to accelerate this quickly, so he hadn't brought a condom with him. He had never been the kind of guy to carry one around 'just in case,' as he wasn't the type to gift his body so freely when the urge took him. No, it took a special man to elicit this kind of reaction from him, and there was no other man like Zee.

John glanced at the bedside drawer and opened it, rummaging around to find a condom. What he found instead was a box. His curiosity got the better of him and he delved in, finding small mementos from Zee's trip around the world. The first thing that caught his attention was a photograph of Zee with someone else, and the thing that struck John the most was how happy they looked together.

Before he could put it back, Zee came back into the room. He stopped short when he saw what John was holding.

"What have you got there? What are you doing?" Zee asked. He marched toward John and snatched the picture out of his hands, burying it deep in the box and slamming the drawer shut.

"I'm sorry," John exclaimed. "I was just looking for a condom and I found that. I was just curious."

"That's private," Zee said sternly. John backed away in fear. He could sense the mood in the room had changed. From sizzling with passion, Zee was now bristling with anger.

"I know, I'm sorry. I wasn't prying, honestly, I was just trying to get ready for you to... you know..." John said in faltering words. "Who is he?"

Zee looked away from him. "I think you should leave," he said, in a voice that was most definitely not one that was going to be argued with. There were many risks John was willing to take, but this wasn't one of them. He rose from the bed and retreated, hoping that he hadn't just ruined his chances completely, and hoping that he just hadn't caused drama for Melissa's wedding.

Chapter Six

Zee stood there feeling betrayed and ashamed. There was a part of him that wanted to call John back and explain everything, while another part just wanted to keep it all locked away. He stared at the drawer. There was a lump in his throat and the energy that had surged within him had shifted to anger. He told himself that he was being stupid for ever thinking he could move on this quickly. It was too soon. As much as he enjoyed John's company he should never have led John on like this. But at the time he thought if he just tried it, if he just gave into the fantasy of it all then maybe it would help to dull the pain. The kiss in the park had been sweet, and when John asked to come up Zee thought it would do him good to force himself to move on. But then John had found a sliver of Zee's past and brought it all crashing down.

There were light footsteps outside his door. Anita stood there. She must have just returned.

"What's going on Zee? Who was that running out of here?" she asked.

"It's nothing Mom. Don't worry."

"Who was he Zee? Are you in trouble?"

"Mom, honestly, it's nothing. I'm not in trouble. I just want to be left alone," he said, striding across the room to slam the door in her face, shutting her out entirely as though he was a brooding teenager. He hated the look he saw just as he shut the door, for he knew that he had just broken her heart. He had already been away for a few years, and even though he was home there was still a part of him that was elsewhere. There were times when he wished he had never come home at all, when he should have just wandered around the rest of the world in search for something he knew he would never find. Maybe his mother would have been better off if he stayed away. At least then she would never have to get a glimpse of how much pain he was in.

***

It was later on in the evening when there was another knock at his bedroom door. Zee had exiled himself in his room. Night had fallen and he was sitting in darkness, sullen and moody, as though if he just ignored the rest of the world then it would all go away. Unfortunately nothing was ever that simple. Anita had come up and tried to offer him dinner, but Zee had ignored her. Each time it was as though he was stabbing both their hearts, for he knew that she was only worried. She deserved a better son than him. Here she was, giving him a shelter and love when all he'd done was desert her.

He didn't dare open the door to get the meal she had left for him in case she heard him and came up. The last thing he wanted was to tell her what had happened. He didn't want to tell anyone. He had spent so long living in solitude, keeping his emotions to himself, and the last time he had opened his heart to become vulnerable it had left him feeling ruined and bitter. Even with John, despite how sweet he was, Zee knew he had to keep things from him. Zee couldn't risk letting himself be so weak again.

There was another knock at the door. This time he knew it wasn't his Mom. It was stronger than that.

"Zee? It's Ryan, come on buddy open up."

Zee pressed his lips together and wished Anita hadn't called Ryan.

"Come on man, your Mom called me. She said you're upset. Just let me in," he said.

Again Zee did not reply. It didn't stop Ryan though. The door came open. The barrier was broached. The castle was stormed and no defense had been adequate to keep Ryan out. Zee glared at him through the darkness, annoyed that his privacy had been summarily dismissed as though it didn't matter at all. Ryan closed the door behind him and switched the light on, bathing the room in an electric glow.

"God it's so dark in here," he said.

"I like it this way. If you didn't get the message I want to be alone," Zee said through gritted teeth. Ryan didn't seem to care.

"Anita is worried about you. She wouldn't have called me if this was fine. Come on Zee, what happened?"

"Nothing happened. It's not a big deal. Nobody needs to worry about me because I'm fine. There's nothing wrong here, I just want to be left alone."

Ryan gave him a patronizing look and John hated it because it was clear that Ryan could see through his lies.

"I can't do that buddy. You wouldn't do the same for me. You're my best man, my best friend. I'm hardly going to leave you alone. If you don't want to talk about anything then that's fine, but I'm not just going to leave you alone. I'll sit here and be quiet if that's what it takes, but I'm not leaving," Ryan said. Zee had been away for a long time, but some things never changed. He knew when there was no point arguing with Ryan, and this was one of those times. Ryan sat on the end of the bed, but he didn't keep his promise to keep quiet.

"Anita said that a guy ran out of here. Who was he?" Ryan asked.

"John," Zee said in a soft voice.

"*John* John?" Ryan asked with arched eyebrows. Zee nodded. "Wow, I didn't think he was your type. I haven't always thought that much of him, but Melissa thinks the world of him so I guess he can't be all bad. But what did you do to scare him off?"

"I didn't do anything," Zee snapped.

Ryan sighed. "You know this isn't going to work if you're not going to be honest with me. I know I haven't always been the best when it comes to dealing with your secrets, but I want to be better and if there's something going on then I'd like to hear about it."

"There's nothing going on," Ryan said, throwing his hands up in the air, but he knew it was a futile thing to declare.

"I think we both know that's not true. Is it about your Dad?"

Zee blanched at this. A shadow fell across his face and he became even more sullen than before.

"It's not about Dad. It's not about anything."
"It has to be about something Zee. You wouldn't act like this otherwise. This isn't you."

"What would you know? I've been gone for years. You don't know what happened to me out there. You don't know what I did. I'm not the same person as when I left. I'm not the person you used to know. Can't you accept that I've changed? I'm sorry I'm not the same guy you remember."

"I know you've changed Zee. That's not what I'm saying. The world didn't make you cruel. The world didn't make you push the people who love you away. Just tell me what's going on. Tell me what happened. Something changed you. Why would you try something with John if you know it wasn't going to lead anywhere? I don't want you to mess up the wedding."

"I thought it might lead somewhere. I thought it might help me get over…" Zee trailed away, worried that he was going to reveal more than he was prepared to, but perhaps it was already too late.

"Get over *what* Zee?" Ryan asked in an exasperated tone.

Zee sat there on his bed, a pitiful figure. For all he had accomplished and all he had experienced throughout his life he had ended up back here, where he had begun. In some ways it felt as though he had not made any progress at all, as though the last few years of his life had been nothing more than a fever dream that left him scarred and traumatized. But despite all this he wasn't left alone. Maybe he didn't think he deserved to be loved. Maybe he didn't think he deserved this kindness and compassion, but that didn't stop Ryan and his mother from sharing it with him. The rest of the world seemed so far away, but all that had happened to him was etched in his heart. All the pain and sorrow he felt he held within him and it was like poison.

Ryan's words lingered in the air. For a terrible moment Zee was about to bite his tongue and keep it all within him, but he knew if he did he might never be able to share anything again. Ryan had been there with him through all his life. If he couldn't trust Ryan with this then he couldn't trust anyone. So, with a voice that cracked under the weight of his emotion and with eyes that glistened with tears, Zee told Ryan exactly what had happened.

***

"Are you sure this is a good idea?" Zee asked in a quiet voice. He was emotionally drained after his conversation with Ryan. When it was over Ryan had asked him honest questions, and Zee had answered him as sincerely as he could. But it wasn't over yet. One of the questions that had been posed by Ryan was if Zee really liked John, or if John was just a distraction to try and save him from his own sorrow. In truth Zee wasn't sure how to answer, but when he thought of John he was filled with happiness and excitement, and a smile appeared on his face. That was all the answer Ryan needed. But he told Zee that John deserved an explanation as well. So now they were sitting outside John's apartment. Ryan had already made the call to Melissa, for she was with John at the moment. Apparently he was upset.

"I didn't mean to get you involved like this," Zee said.

"I know you'll be there for me when Melissa and I have an argument," he replied.

"Aren't you supposed to be looking on the bright side? Why would you assume that you're going to have arguments?"

"It's the married life, isn't it? Some things are inevitable," Ryan replied. Zee wasn't sure whether he was being pragmatic or fatalistic, but he had too much else on his mind to worry about that at the moment. He took a deep breath and then summoned his courage. Ryan wished him good luck as Zee stepped out of the car. He walked up to the apartment and knocked on the door. Melissa opened.

"Be kind to him," she said, and then they swapped places. Melissa went back to her fiancé, while Ryan went inside the apartment.

He found John sitting on the couch. A bottle of wine had been shared between him and Melissa, although it looked as though she had had more than her fair share. The mood in the air was tense. Zee wasn't exactly sure what to say as it had been a while since he had been involved with someone like this, and the last time he'd had a difficult conversation it hadn't ended well.

"I'm sorry for what happened earlier. I didn't mean to react that way it's just that you... well... you caught me by surprise," Zee said.

John looked pensive. His gaze darted toward Zee, but it never settled on the man. He didn't ask Zee to sit down either. While Zee didn't want to assume that he was a welcome guest, he also didn't want to stand up while John was sitting, as it made him seem more imposing and he wasn't trying to intimidate anyone.

"I thought we were having a good time," John said quietly.

"We were," Zee said.

"What was it all about? I just don't know how you could go from being so hot to so cold so quickly. I was all ready to... you know... but then you just switched like that," he snapped his fingers.

"I know. I'm sorry. I didn't mean for it to be like that."

"I haven't had the most experience when it comes to relationships, but I don't expect to be treated like that," John said. "And I know things got pretty hot and heavy there, but I don't want to just fall into bed with someone. I want to get to know them properly. That's why I was looking in the drawer in the first place, because I don't carry a condom with me. I wasn't prying. I'm sorry if it came across that way."

"No, John, you don't have anything to apologize for. I overreacted. I'm sorry. And I'm sorry for getting so intense so quickly as well. I'm not usually like that I just... in all honesty I'm a bit of a mess right now and I thought if I could force myself to get that far with you then maybe it would help me move on," Zee said as he leaned forward, clasping his hands together in between his open legs. John held his body tight and narrow, as if to shield himself from any further harm.

"Move on from what?" John asked.

This was the moment, Zee thought. He opened his mouth and took a deep breath, but the moments passed before he could bring himself to talk about it. It was one thing to tell Ryan, but another to tell John.

"Is it about the guy in the photo?" John asked.

Zee nodded slowly and tried to swallow a lump that appeared in his throat, but it wouldn't go away.

"Who is he?"

"His name is Adam and I loved him," Zee said.

"I see," John said coldly. "I thought it might be something like that. Do you still love him now?"

Zee sighed. He had asked himself that question so many times and was yet to come up with an adequate answer. "I think in a way I'm always going to love him, or at least the time we spent together. But no, I'm not in love with him. That all disappeared when I left. Now there's just... well... grief I suppose."

"It sounds like it was intense."

"It was," Zee said. He shifted in his seat, aware that this was probably uncomfortable for John. It was definitely uncomfortable for Zee. It was never nice to speak about the ex-lover of someone you were interested in, especially not when there were still strong feelings whirring around.

"What happened with him? How did you meet?"

Zee started by speaking slowly, for reliving these memories was a difficult thing to do. Each one was like peeling away a band aid, revealing a raw and unhealed wound underneath.

"He was backpacking across the world, much like me. We met in a hostel once and just got to talking. We ended up hanging out together and since he had no direction he decided to tag along with me. People like to say that I'm a free spirit, but he really embodies the concept. He never regretted leaving anything behind."

"Is that why you hurt so much? Did he leave you behind?" John asked.

Zee shook his head. "It was me who did the leaving. We'd been together for a while. We'd seen a lot of different things together and been to a lot of different places. We used to talk about the future and how we were going to comb through every part of the world to find the hidden secrets that nobody else discovered. He hated the modern world and everything that came with it. What he wanted more than anything was to disappear into nature and not have to worry about the trappings of society. At the time I was of a similar mind, although I was still tethered to the world by my job. I wasn't ready to let it go just yet. Anyway, when we came to different cities I checked my emails and letters and things, and one day I learned that my father had died. I wasn't sure how to feel at the time. I spoke to Adam about it and he acted like it was something to be celebrated. He said that it was a sign that I should leave the world behind because there wasn't really anything left for me any longer."

"That sounds pretty horrible," John said.

"I thought so too at the time, even though he was everything to me. It was as though he changed in that moment, and he was never going to be the same again. I told him that I couldn't stay away from home. I had to get there for my Mom and to say goodbye to my Dad. I had already missed so much. I was prepared to miss anymore."

"I'm guessing Adam didn't feel the same way."

Zee shook his head, and his words took on an even heavier tone. "He did not. I thought he might have shown some sympathy for me, or at least some pity. He was never fazed by anything, and he expected the same of me. I couldn't be like him though. I needed to come home. He begged me to stay. He called me a coward. He insulted me. Then he said he was sorry and begged me to go around the world with him. He said that the best tribute I could pay to my father would be to stick to my dreams. But I couldn't. I told him that maybe in the future I would come back, if he wanted to wait for me. I said that he could even come back with me, but the thought was like poison to him. He said that he had escaped society once and he wasn't going to be pulled back again, not even for love. Then he said that love was just a trick as well. He walked away from me when I was in tears and told me that I was a fool and a fraud for leading him on. He said that the world didn't belong to me because I couldn't surrender to it wholly and completely, and that I was no better than a tourist."

It took John some time to process what Zee told him. "I know this all means a lot to you, but he sounds like a jerk. Who acts like that to someone who has just lost their father?"

"I know. I know I should hate him and I know that I shouldn't let the good times we shared cloud the fact that he treated me terribly, but it felt like I lost more than my father. I ended up with nothing left except memories. Maybe if I hadn't met Adam I would have returned home a little earlier and spent some time with Dad before he died, or maybe if Dad hadn't died I would have spent more time with Adam. It just feels like I lost so much and I didn't get anything in return.

When I came back here I told myself that I needed some time to get a handle on things again. I didn't expect to meet anyone I liked, or anyone that would like me. I wanted to give things a go with you, to try and force myself into the state of mind where I can move on, but when I saw you looking at the picture... I don't know... it just felt as though these two parts of my life were crashing together and all I wanted to do was keep them separate. It wasn't the most mature way to handle it and I'm sorry for shouting at you and acting so irrationally."

Zee said all this with looking at John as little as possible, for he was filled with shame when he thought about how he had treated John. He wouldn't have been offended or surprised if John had asked him to leave there and then, but John was patient and responded with kind words.

"I know what it's like to feel like this," he said. "Love can mess you up inside and it's never easy. I think it's good that you even tried to move on with me. I've always been the opposite. I've been so scared of being hurt again that I find it hard to try anything."

"Is that why you were so nervous when you told me that you liked me?" Zee asked.

John nodded. "It all goes back to a time in high school. I was pretty lonely and Melissa thought I should find a boyfriend, which was easier said than done. Now, our school was pretty progressive and there were some other guys who were out, but it wasn't like there was a club or anything. There was this guy, Lenny, who was always the life and soul of the party. There was something about him that I just couldn't get out of my mind. I was absolutely floored by him, and one day I made the mistake of telling Melissa. All she wanted was the best for me and I think it says a lot about her that she didn't see why he wouldn't like me. She tried to get me to go up to him, but I just wouldn't do it. All I could think about was stammering in front of him, and him looking at me like I was crazy."

"So what happened?"

Melissa convinced me that everything was going to be okay and it was just my own insecurity that was preventing me from asking him out. She told me that she was going to help me, and the way she acted she seemed to think it was a foregone conclusion that he was going to say yes. Despite my doubts I trusted her, because that's just the way Melissa is. Anyway, so one day before class starts we're sitting there waiting for the teacher and then Lenny comes in. I'm starting to sweat like crazy now and all I want to do is stop this before it begins, but Melissa has already waved Lenny over and she tells him that I have a little crush on him and she wants to know if he'd think about going out with me.

I'll never forget the look on his face. There was a moment when I thought he might actually say yes, but then he just laughed. He taunted me and asked Melissa if she was joking because there was no way he was going to go out with someone like me. His friends laughed too and everyone else in the class just sat there and stared at me. I heard the whispers. I could feel the way they just felt so awful for me. Melissa told me that she was sorry. The worst part was I couldn't even leave because then the teacher came in and began the lesson. I had to sit there on the verge of tears and hope that he didn't ask me to say anything. Meanwhile Lenny was sitting there so close to me, not caring at all that he had just humiliated me. I ran home and cried. It took a while for Melissa to make it up to me, but ever since then I've just been afraid of revealing my feelings because I end up getting hurt. So when the same thing happened today it just... I don't know... it made me feel really shitty."

"I'm sorry you had to go through that. I'm sorry for reminding you about it today as well. I never wanted this to happen. I just think I'm such a mess. This is why I thought about not coming home at all, because when you come home people have expectations of you and they want you to be a certain way. I'm not sure I can be like that anymore. I lost something out there and I'm not sure I can get it back."

The words were somber and depressing. Whenever Zee felt like this it was as though there was nothing but darkness and despair around him. The shadows were long and tall, and there was no daylight shining through the bleak clouds. He thought he would have been able to keep up a brave face for longer than he had done, although perhaps that had been too much to ask. At least he had been honest with John though. Maybe they could still be friends.

Chapter Seven

John listened to everything Zee had to say with an open mind. He still wanted to give John the benefit of the doubt despite everything. He had poured his heart out to Melissa and she had tried to reassure him, although she wasn't very convincing. Apparently Ryan had told her that Zee wanted to make it up to John. It was kind of them to work together to try and help John, but he wasn't sure how effective it would be. He had expected another man to be involved, but the story Zee told him had been one of heartache and misery. John had known his fair share of jerks throughout the years, and it seemed as though Zee had fallen prey to one of them as well.

But the mere fact that Zee had actually opened up to John meant a lot. The hardest thing for John had been the shunning, the closed door after everything had seemed open to him. He could feel the pain in Zee's words, and the last thing he wanted was for Zee to feel like there was no way out.

"I know you might feel as though you lost something that you might never get back, but that doesn't mean you have. And it doesn't mean you can't find something here either. What you've been through... it's just another heartache. I've let those get the better of me before as well. But one thing I also know from experience is that you shouldn't force yourself into doing something that you're not ready for either, because it's only going to lead to... well... situations like today. It's okay, my ego can take a bit of a bruising now and then. If you're not that into me then you should just take some time to yourself. Life isn't a race and there's no deadline to these things."

"That's not what I came here to say John. I know it's confusing right now, but I wouldn't have kissed you if I didn't want to, and I wouldn't have taken you into my home if I didn't want you to be there either. You weren't wrong when you said that there was something between us and what you told me at the park... I feel the same way. I've really enjoyed spending time with you and I just wish I was better at this kind of thing. Out there in the wild when it's just me and my camera... life can seem so simple. When other people get involved it gets complicated."

"Yeah, I know what that's like. For the longest time I've been living vicariously through Melissa. I haven't been able to work up the courage to take a risk," John said, blushing slightly. "But I promise you that I'm not here to make your life complicated."

Zee nodded. Every word they said was hesitant. John could feel that they were on the precipice of something monumental, and he didn't want to do anything to jeopardize it. It was as though he was a hunter sneaking up on skittish prey and one wrong move would send it scurrying away, never to be seen again. Life was made up of chances, and John was always afraid that he would run out of them.

"So where do you want to go from here? Can I consider myself forgiven?" Zee asked.

John smirked. "I'm not sure I can let you off that easily. I think I'd be doing myself a disservice if I didn't insist you take me out for a drink or an ice cream or something."

"I get that," Zee said, smiling.

"But what do you think you can handle? I mean, do you just want to be friends?"

"How about we just keep getting to know each other and see how it goes?" Zee suggested. It wasn't exactly what John was hoping to hear, but it was certainly better than nothing, and it was much improved from what he thought things were going to be like when he had left Zee's place.

"That sounds good to me, for now," John said. "But will you answer a question I have... the way you've been so reticent to talk about your travels, is it because of Adam?"

John noticed the way Zee winced whenever the name of that man was mentioned, and John knew that things must have been serious if the name still had this much of an effect. He nodded and looked ashamed.

"Maybe you should tell me about some of these experiences then," John said. "It might help for you to bring them home, so to speak, rather than forever be associated with Adam."

Zee seemed to think this was a good idea so they spent the rest of the night talking about everything Zee had experienced. John was an attentive listener and after some moments of awkwardness Zee relaxed into the stories. They came one after the other. Some of them Zee had almost forgotten himself, and it was a joy to relive them again. John found Zee's story compelling and he only wished that he had been a part of this period of his life. But he wondered what stories might be told in the future, and what role he might have to play in them. They were so lost in each other's company that neither of them realized they had been talking all night until dawn's rosy fingers reached in through the windows and bathed them in a golden glow.

It was the first night they had spent together, but it would not be the last. For now though John was content at having this man in his life. Taking it slow suited him given his past, and he was sure that everything would be worth the wait.

Chapter Eight

Months had passed since Zee had been at one of his lowest points. He was grateful to Ryan and John for saving him, and from that point it had only been a steady rise to something approaching happiness. He had spoken with Anita as well to let her know what was going on with him, and it had brought them closer together. Now John and he did not have to use wedding planning as an excuse to hang out either. They went out for drinks, watched movies, and spent plenty of time together. But Zee did find it difficult to break fully away from the past. There were moments when they came close to kissing again, but neither of them were sure that it was the right moment. Zee wondered if the time would come again for them to be close, or if they had just missed their opportunity.

It didn't help that as they got closer, Melissa and Ryan were having problems. John had tried to warn Zee that an argument was inevitable because that was their nature, but Zee thought he was being dramatic. However, when it came it hit like a storm. One evening he was enjoying a peaceful night alone when Ryan came around with a face like thunder. He was ranting and raving and basically telling Zee that the wedding wasn't going to be happening any longer. Zee listened patiently and tried to get him to calm down, but Ryan was adamant. All the while Zee wondered if John was experiencing the same thing with Melissa.

"I never even wanted to get married in the first place," Ryan yelled. "I'm doing all of this for her and she's being difficult about it. I don't know what more I have to do. Sometimes I think she's so ungrateful."

Zee listened without trying to pass judgment as he knew that would only make Ryan more upset. Eventually Zee told Ryan to go back home and watch some football, and that he would talk to John and try to sort it out. It was his duty as the best man to make the wedding go ahead after all. He could tell from John's tone that John was beleaguered by the ordeal as well, but he agreed to meet anyway.

Zee gave him a dry smile when John entered. Whenever Zee saw John he was reminded of the moment when they kissed, and he wondered if such a moment would ever come again. They had spent a lot of time together and shared so many feelings, yet Zee feared he had missed the opportunity to make more of it. They were in a strange sort of limbo now where neither of them seemed willing to make the next move. Zee understood why John wouldn't want to take the risk again because had already been spurned and likely didn't want to become vulnerable. For his part Zee was still unsure how much of himself he could give to John, and he didn't want to take a step too far and end up hurting John. So the two of them danced around their true feelings without really acknowledging them. They were more than friends, less than lovers, and Zee wasn't entirely sure if or when they were going to make a decision.

But for now they had more important things to worry about.

"So how's Melissa doing?" Zee asked as he welcomed John into his room. Anita was out for the day at work.

John sighed. "She's about as well as she can be I suppose. There are moments when she seems calm, but then she'll think about what happened again and she explodes with anger. I'm not sure I've ever seen her this pissed off before. How is Ryan?" Zee noticed the edge in John's words. It seemed as though the enmity that existed between the two men had only thawed rather than disappeared entirely. Zee pressed his lips together. His natural instinct was to come to the defense of his best friend, but he also had to navigate this conversation deftly.

"Ryan is Ryan. He just wants everything to be settled again."

"Well maybe he should have thought of that before this happened," John said sharply.

"I think Melissa could give him a chance to explain. It's not like he actually did anything," Zee said.

John looked at him with disbelief. "Wait a minute, you don't actually think that, do you? Surely you can't be on his side?"

"I mean, I think he was a bit stupid, but he's not cruel. He just had a bit too much to drink, that's all. And it's not like he hid it from Melissa either. He told her straight away."

"But he flirted with another woman and got her number! That's not normal behavior. If he does this now what's to stop him doing it when they're married?"

"Ryan is many things but he's not a cheat. He loves Melissa too much to do that to her."

"That's not what I heard," John said under his breath.

"What's that supposed to mean?" Zee asked sternly.

"I've heard about what he was like at school, always parading a string of women around and dumping them whenever it got serious."

"Yeah and that was a long time ago. He's not the same guy. Just the fact that he's getting married to Melissa should be enough to prove that."

"It's not. Now she's worried that he hasn't changed as much as she thought he had. You and Ryan can't just brush this away as an innocent mistake. Why didn't he tell this girl that he was engaged?"

A shadow fell across Zee's face. "Look man I'm not saying that Ryan is blameless in all this, I'm just saying that maybe Melissa could chill out a little bit. She's not doing anyone any favors by shutting things down like this. Ryan told her what happened, he apologized, and he didn't even reply to that girl. There's not a crime against being friendly."

"There is when you're in a relationship. There are certain standards and Ryan has failed to meet them," John said, sounding so impassioned as though it was he who had been hurt rather than Melissa. Zee bit his tongue regarding what he was about to say next as he didn't want to make John even angrier. He took a breath and reminded himself that this wasn't about proving innocent or guilt, but rather about getting to a point where Melissa and Ryan could get back on track.

"All I'm saying is that maybe Melissa should accept Ryan's explanation and not get so afraid of what might happen in the future. I know Ryan better than anyone and I can see how much he loves Melissa. He's never felt this way about a girl before and he's not going to do anything to jeopardize it. If he didn't care this much then he wouldn't have even been tempted to tell her. She has to take that into account."

"She doesn't have to take anything into account. She has to protect herself," John said.

There was something about the way he said it that rankled Zee. His skin prickled, as though there was an itch that he couldn't scratch, and his lips curled into a snarl.

"Is that her talking or is that you planting ideas in her head?" he asked, his words as heavy as hammers.

John looked at him, his expression of shock turning into one of dismay almost immediately. "What are you talking about?"

"You know what I'm talking about. You have a big thing about being hurt because of what happened, and you've never really liked Ryan. You've only ever put up with him because Melissa has been in love with him. I'm just wondering if you've been waiting for a chance to sabotage it."

"What the hell? How could you even think that?"

"I've gotten to know you pretty well over the past few months John and I think I know what you're scared of and what you don't like. When Melissa and Ryan get married things are going to change for you. You won't be able to rely on Melissa as much, so this is the perfect opportunity for you to try and convince her that marriage isn't a good idea. She can go back to square one and you can keep things the way they are."

The words flew from Zee's mouth like arrows, and every one hit their target without any error. John's face turned a shade of crimson and he began to tremble with anger. Regret soared through Zee's heart, but it was too late to take the words back.

"How dare you say that! The only thing I want for Melissa is for her to be happy, and to be honest yes, I have often questioned whether she can be happy with Ryan. But what would you know about that? You haven't been here to see the day to day life of their relationship. I've been there to dry the tears, and I've lost count of how many tears there have been. They're not some perfect couple, and I'm not going to tell my best friend that things are going to be all right when they aren't. Ryan really needs to look inside himself and ask him if he can act like a husband should act, because Melissa doesn't deserve anything but the best, and she's not going to settle for anything lesser either."

"Well I think she's setting her sights too high then. People aren't perfect John. They make mistakes, and no relationship happens without someone getting hurt along the way, but that doesn't mean things are over."

"Yeah, a punching bag would say that," John said darkly. Zee wasn't the only one whose words were barbed. Zee recoiled. His heart swam and his throat tightened. Suddenly he wished that he hadn't invited John over at all. The air between them was warm. The glare in John's eyes was icy, and it felt as though they were fighting for Ryan and Melissa rather than trying to resolve the situation.

"What the hell did you just call me?" Zee asked.

"You heard me. You might be used to having someone walk all over you in a relationship, but that's not the way normal people deal with things. If they're mistreated then they walk away and look for someone to treat them better, they don't mope around and get depressed about someone who never loved them in the first place."

John looked utterly drained when he said this, as though he had just reached deep inside himself and yanked out all of his anguished emotions, leaving them bare and on display for everyone to see. And it was at that moment when Zee realized this argument wasn't about Ryan and Melissa at all.

"So that's what this is about," Zee said, folding his arms.

John averted his gaze. "I don't know what you mean. I'm here to try and sort things out between Melissa and Ryan. We have to get the wedding back on track."

"Screw the wedding," Zee said. "You clearly have something on your mind, so you'd better tell me now. Isn't being honest with each other how 'normal' people handle things in a relationship?" he challenged. John shifted his weight uncomfortably from foot to foot and looked as though he wanted the world to swallow him whole, but to his credit he did not try to retreat or equivocate. Instead he seemed to understand that it was inevitable this was going to happen. They had been caught in a whirlwind storm of emotion and there was no way out.

"Fine, you want me to be honest? I'll be honest," John said. "I don't understand why you've been so invested in the past when the past hurt you. I don't get why you're still moping over Adam when all he did was turn his back and hurt you. I don't get why I'm not enough for you to move on. I've given you time. I've given you space, but it never seems as though it's going to lead anywhere. I don't know what more I can do. I don't know if this is even going anywhere. I still like you, but I don't know if you're actually here or not. Is there any point in me having feelings for you? I just don't get why you'd feel this way about Adam and not about me when I would never treat you like this. Why can't you just get over him?"

"You know it's not that easy," Zee said, although now it was his turn for the blood to rush around his body. He grit his teeth and his hands clenched into tight balls by his side. "It's been a difficult time."

"But don't you ever want it to be over? I mean what are we doing here?" John asked, stretching his hands out limply.

"I don't know," Zee said.

"After we talked about this I thought that things were going to go somewhere, but they never have. Have you changed your mind, or were you just never that interested in me in the first place?"

"I don't know!" Zee exclaimed, probably more loudly than he anticipated. "I don't know," he repeated, this time more quietly. "Since I've come back I haven't been sure of who I am. I can't stop thinking about what happened in the past and I just... I don't know if I can give you everything you want, everything you deserve. I don't want to hurt you John. You're a sensitive guy. I don't want to ruin your life."

"You're hurting me already," John said in a soft whisper.

"I didn't mean to," Zee confessed. "I just... I've been such a mess. I thought I'd be out of it by now, but I guess it's taking longer than I thought."

"I thought you'd be done with it as well. You know I'm not a kid anymore. I have a thick skin. You don't have to molly coddle me. If you're not interested then you can just say so. I'm not going to make a scene, and I'm not going to make things awkward for the wedding."

"You're missing the point John. I *am* interested in you," Zee said.

"Then why haven't you done anything about it? I'm right here Zee. I've always been right here. You keep saying you want to move on, so prove it and move on. You're not traveling around the world anymore. You're not with Adam anymore. This is where you are. This is where you exist. You have to start living here, otherwise you're never going to move on."

The words struck a chord in Zee's heart. He looked at John earnestly and realized that he was speaking the truth. Ever since Zee had been at home he had cocooned himself in this false youth that he thought would protect him, but instead it had only let the pain fester. The one brief glimmer of hope before had been when he and John had come close to making love, but even then Zee's pain had ruined that. He kept blaming the past for hurting him and for keeping him from being happy, but in truth he knew that the path was just a nebulous concept and it only had a hold on his life because he allowed it to have a hold on his life.

Well now was the time to change.

There were moments in a person's life that defined who they were and what their future was going to be. Zee knew that this moment was one example of this. He had traveled around the world. He had left everything he knew behind in search of adventure, yet somewhere along the way he had lost that vibrant spark of life. But now he had the chance to seize something again. John was here, alive and beautiful and offering himself to Zee. He was sweet and kind and patient, and he wasn't afraid to tell Zee the truth either. Zee knew he would have been mad to let him walk away again. He couldn't let anything stop him from grasping the present with two tight hands, because if he did then he would never escape the shadowy realm of his own regret.

In one burst of vibrant and intense desire Zee took a stride forward, immediately and inexorably closing the distance between him and John. His arms were around John, his lips were upon him. They were lost in a world of heavy breaths and hot desire and bodies that surged with passion. John was shocked at the immediacy of the kiss and yelped at first, but he soon sank into the pleasure of it all. Zee pulled him close, feeling the warm comfort that came from another body, feeling the hard arousal pressing into him. Their kiss deepened. Their tongues danced. Their arms wrapped around each other like coiling vines that tightened and tightened until there was no air between them at all.

They took a moment to catch their breath. Their chests heaved and their breath swirled in their air, their lips so close that their exhalations became one. John's eyes sparkled with wonder. The intensity of the argument had unlocked something inside Zee. The corners of his lips twitched into a smile and then he went in for another kiss. He ran his hands through John's hair and one hand went to the small of John's back. Time seemed to stand still and the world melted away. Suddenly all of Zee's pain and torment didn't seem to matter any longer. There was only John. There was only happiness. There was only lust.

Zee ran his hands down John's body and clasped both his hands, squeezing them gently.

"I'm sorry for the way I've been acting and for the things I said. I haven't meant to neglect you," Zee said softly, pressing his forehead against John's.

"I'm sorry too. I didn't mean to be so cruel I just... I'm sorry if I'm pushing you too much."

"I think I might need a little pushing. You're right. I have been too lost in the past. I need to think about what's right in front of me and what's going to be there in the future." Zee squeezed John's hands again when he said this and then plucked another soft kiss from John's lips. Each kiss was warmer and sweeter than the last. Each one elicited another surge of burning desire within Zee, and he was beginning to remember all the good things that rode on love's wings rather than the pain and bitterness that had been tangled in his heart. Like a cluster of black clouds that were blown away by a light summer breeze, so too did Zee's heart become brighter in John's presence. When he realized this he smiled widely, although there was still a touch of reservation.

"I feel like I've wasted so much time already. If I had just done this when we had first kissed..." he began, trailing away.

"Then let's just make up for it now. We still have plenty of time left," John said.

Zee did not need any further invitation. They kissed again and then he led John upstairs to his room. The door closed behind them and the mattress creaked gently as they sank to the bed in a tangle of limbs and lips. They descended into murmurs and laughs and long, soft kisses. They let their hands roam about each other's bodies, getting used to the feelings and the contours. They peeled away each other's clothes, gradually exposing their flesh inch by inch.

Their tops were thrown to the floor first, creating a puddle of unwanted fabric. They lay side by side, their arms wrapped around each other. John's hand idly traced circles up and down Zee's body as they shared more intimate kisses. It had been a long time since either of them had been intimate with anyone else. For Zee the last time had been in a far different environment in this; he had been on a beach when the sun was setting. The ocean lapped near his feet and it was as though the world smiled on the glory of his love, but now he was in a cramped, private room, the room where he had left all of his childhood awkwardness behind, with this man who had seen nothing more of the world. Yet because of this man this place was just as special as any beach or any meadow that Zee had ever been too.

"You know the first time I saw you I thought you were so hot," Zee murmured in between kisses.

"I felt the same. I couldn't believe my luck. I thought I was going to be torturing myself through the planning of the wedding. I didn't think that someone like you would be interested in someone like me."

"I hope you believe it now. Maybe this will give you a better idea," Zee said, taking John's hand and thrusting it halfway down his body, sending it into the hard chasm of his groin. John groaned at the feeling of Zee's arousal, and Zee felt a wave of pleasure rush through him. He arched his neck back as John started to fumble with the pants, pulling them away with ease. He wriggled out of his own too and more clothes were added to the puddle on the floor. Zee looked down at their bodies, at their manhood. They stood tall and strong. Their bodies bristled with desire. Zee couldn't take his eyes off John's erection. His hand shot down immediately to touch him, and John's hand returned the favor. They lay there, kissing softly as they pleasured each other, feeling the throbbing heat against their palms. The air was seared with desire and Zee thought his heart was going to burst out of his chest. His entire body thrummed with pleasure. Tingles danced all the way down to his feet, as though waves of electricity were pulsing through him.

Then John shifted his body and twisted so that he was atop Zee. There was one long, deep kiss before John began a descent down Zee's body. He left a trail of kisses before he reached Zee's erection. A rush of breath coated him, the warm air rippling across his naked flesh before suddenly two soft lips were wrapped around the sensitive tip, dragging down the shaft until the thick inches disappeared. Zee's vision blurred as the pleasure was so intense. John swirled his tongue and sucked deep and slow, moaning deeply as he did so, managing to take every inch of Zee in his mouth. Zee's body tensed and his hand rested on the back of John's head, feeling the rising motions as John bobbed up and down. Waves of pleasure surged through Zee. He couldn't remember being this hard before, and this much pleasure was certainly enough to vanquish the memory of heartbreak. He could feel everything surging through his body. It was pure and primal and passionate. The air swirled in a thick miasma and the world seemed to lurch and twist, as though everything was dancing around him. John continued to suck, gorging himself on Zee's masculinity until Zee could feel himself on the cusp of pleasure, but he wasn't ready yet.

He pulled John away and kissed him deeply, tasting the hot musk left on hips lips. Then he pinned John on his back and started to pleasure him. He curled his fingers around John's cock and started to jerk him off so quickly that his hand was just a blur.

Then he drifted down John's body and placed a soft kiss upon the tip, before letting a line of saliva drizzle upon the erection, making it glisten and shine. Zee loved the sound of John's moans as he mirrored what John had done earlier, but then the moans became sharper and deeper as something else happened. Zee surreptitiously wet his fingers and then let them slide down between John's legs, finding the warm secret area. John squirmed and writhed, but the moans that leaped from his mouth were ardent and high-pitched. Zee fell into the natural rhythms of his body and curled his finger back and forth slowly, as well as making circular motions that seemed to drive John crazy. He trembled and shuddered and it was all a joy for Zee, who loved watching this kaleidoscopic emotion play upon John's face. He'd almost forgotten how much he loved making another man feel good.

This body of John's was like an instrument, and Zee was quickly become a maestro. He learned the secret sweet spots that made John gasp. He found the areas that no other man had found before. Sweat prickled on his body and trickled down the angles of his muscles, and he could feel the tension in John's body rise to unbearable levels. John grabbed the sheets, his hands curling into fists as the pleasure became too much to bear. The guttural moans crashed through the room, one after the other in a rampant march. Zee glanced up and saw that John's face was clenched in tormented ecstasy, and Zee loved every minute of it. He continued to suck, dragging his tongue up and down John's cock, while his finger still worked furiously inside John's body.

Then came the cry that Zee had been waiting for. What followed was a great tremor, a quake that shook the world. He held John's body as steady as he could and braced himself from the onslaught of warmth that filled his mouth. It came in a great torrent, splashing against his tongue and the back of his throat. It was hot and steaming with lust, and it tasted delicious. As soon as Zee had a good mouthful he pulled himself up and twisted John around, for he was at breaking point and he wasn't sure how long he could hold everything inside for.

He clamped his hands around John's hips. John was still reeling from the orgasm that had hit him like a freight train and groaned as he was bent over. Zee slowly entered him, enjoying the tightness and the heat and the feeling of their bodies melting together in this glorious union, to the point at which it was impossible to tell where one of them ended and the other began. Zee's body glistened with aroused sweat as he let his body fall into a natural thrusting motion. He threw his head back and allowed his instincts to take hold, surrendering his rational mind to something more primal and primitive, letting the natural sensations guide him to a place of bliss. It was as though he transcended his body, his soul becoming lighter than air, and yet he could not escape the searing heat of his flesh, or the rampant desire that flowed within him. With every thrust the passion grew to a more intense height and it was as though the physical and spiritual parts of him were inextricably linked, and the most potent ingredient was John. Without him there would have been no edge to the pleasure, no raging inferno that threatened to tear him apart. It all pulsed and throbbed inside him and he could feel it careening unstoppably, as though ribbons unfurled within him. As he got closer and closer to climax his hands dug deeper into John's flesh. His hips moved with thunder and there was no stopping him at all as the world seemed to tear itself apart and everything rushed out of him in one hot torrent.

Every muscle in his body seized at once as he plunged over the brink of ecstasy and it all released in a bursting supernova that left him drained. All the strength and all the energy rushed out of him in erratic thrusts, and then there was nothing left but hollow breaths as he collapsed to the softness of the sheets, utterly drained and delirious. Stars burst around his head and he looked to the ceiling in a daze as John draped himself over Zee's chest. They were slick with sweat and they lay there in silence as they both processed what they had just experienced, for it had been mind blowing for them both.

***

As the afterglow of sex faded and the men caught their breath, Zee lazily kissed John on the head. They were sticky and hot, but Zee wouldn't have wanted to be anywhere else.

"Well… I guess that helps to relieve some tension," John said softly.

"It sure does," Zee agreed. "And I hope it helps to make up a little for lost time as well."

"It does. So I mean… how do you want to proceed? Like, do you want to actually date or do you just want to keep this to be a casual thing? I know we got a little carried away there…"

"We sure did," Zee said, chuckling to himself. "I don't want to be casual with you John. I don't want you to think that I'm not committed to you. I know my head has been something of a mess, but being with you like that… it really shows me what I've been missing. I know now that I've been stupid to let the past get in the way of my happiness and I don't want that to happen again. You don't have to worry about that," he said. In fact..."

Zee leaned over and plucked the picture of him and Adam out of the box in the drawer by the side of his bed. He took it in his hands and went to rip it apart, but John stopped him at the last moment.

"Are you sure you want to do this?" John said.

"Yes. This is my past. And you're right John. I shouldn't have put so much of my heart into someone who treated me like that. I was blind to what life could be. I need to look forward. The past is the past and it's always going to stay there. It's time to make new memories."

John took his hand away. Zee tore the picture in half and let it fall to the floor. Then he turned back to John and kissed him, embracing everything that was in his present, and everything that might be in his future too. But then John's face fell.

"What's wrong?" Zee asked.

"It's just... I'm thinking about Ryan and Melissa. We came here to try and sort things out between them, to save the marriage. I'm happy that this happened, but we're supposed to be there for our friends."

"I'm sure we can help them sort it out. But we can't just live for them. We have to live for ourselves too," Zee said.

Chapter Nine

"Do you really think this is a good idea?" Melissa asked. She and John were sitting in a spa, relaxing with a cocktail beside them and soothing ointments on their skin. They were alone. Melissa said she wanted to do this with John and John alone, while a hen night with her other friends and family could follow later. From the tone of her voice John knew that she wasn't talking about anything in the spa, but rather about the marriage itself. The ceremony was only days away. It had been months since the last huge argument, the argument that had almost caused a rift between him and Zee as well as Melissa and Ryan. But all four of them had pulled through it.

"I do," John said.

"Even though Ryan is... well... Ryan?" Melissa asked.

"I know we've had our differences in the past and my opinion hasn't always been that high of him, but the fact is that he has always been honest with you and he made the step of proposing to you because he realizes that you're going to be the best thing that ever happens to him. I trust Zee when he says that Ryan won't do anything to hurt you. And if you think that Ryan is the best thing that can happen to you then..."

"I do love him. I know you might not understand why, but I do."

John smiled. "Sometimes love doesn't need to be understood. It just needs to be experienced."

"That's very wise of you to say. Look at you, you've been in a relationship for a few months and you think you know everything," she flashed him a wry smile. John chuckled.

"I wouldn't go that far, but I do understand what you've been going through more now. Things with Zee didn't start off easy, but it was worth the drama to get to the good stuff," he said.

"So things are good between the two of you?"

"Oh yeah. They're really great. Better than I though they'd be actually. It's just... it makes me wonder why it was so hard to find anyone to love me before. Like... things are so easy with Zee I don't understand why it had to be so hard with anyone else."

"That's a sign that he's the right one for you. The thing is even though Ryan and I have had our troubles, it's never been a hard relationship. Like, when we've been able to come back we've always been able to sort it out."

"Are you willing to go through that for the rest of your life though? I mean, it's not as though being married is going to change the way the two of you are, is it? The nature of your relationship is going to be the same. I don't want to pour cold water on things, but is that something you're prepared for?"

Melissa thought about it for a moment and then gave a swift nod of her head. "Maybe it's not what everyone would want, but I guess I know that Ryan is always going to come back to me. I know he wouldn't have asked me to get married if he didn't truly mean it. It's so out of character for what he wanted before I just... it's a huge gesture. To be honest I thought he'd be freaking out more before the wedding, but he seems to have gotten used to the idea of getting married. I daresay he's even excited about it."

"Of course he is. He's marrying the most beautiful woman in the world," John said. Melissa laughed and they clinked their glasses together, toasting to the happy occasion.

"I just can't believe it's all going to be over soon. All this planning… all for one day. Sometimes I wonder if it's all worth it."

"Of course it is. It's going to be a day you're never going to forget, and if you hadn't decided to get married I might never have met Zee either."

"This is true. And at least I don't have to bother with plus ones for either of you since you're going to be coming together."

John chuckled. "That is a plus."

"Just please don't have a dramatic fight or something on the day," she said in a warning tone.

"You know I would never do that to you, and Zee wouldn't do that to Ryan either. It's going to be a wonderful day and there are only going to be happy memories at the end of it. I just don't know what I'm going to do with myself when you're on your honeymoon. I don't think we've ever been apart from each other for that long," John said.

"No, we haven't. It's going to be strange. I suppose there are going to be other things that change as well as we go through life."

An uneasy feeling swam in the pit of his stomach as he thought about the future. So many things had changed already, and while some of them were good changes, he wasn't sure that he was ready for more. And there was one big change that had been playing on his mind, something that he and Melissa hadn't spoken about before, but the closer the wedding came the more difficult it was to ignore.

"Have you and Ryan spoken about children?" he asked.

"We have," Melissa said. "But I don't think we're planning on having one yet. We just want to get the wedding out of the way first and see what happens from there. There's only so much change I can take."

John breathed a sigh of relief as he didn't want things to change too much too quickly.

"I'm glad that you've found someone who has made you happy," Melissa said. "It's about time it happened." She flashed him a reassuring smile and then she sighed a little. "I have to admit that I'm a little worried about Ryan's stag party."

"How come?"

"You know what Ryan is like. I'm worried that something crazy is going to happen and there's going to be some other drama."

John shook his head. "I spoke with Zee and he assured me that isn't going to be the case. He told me that he's not going to put Ryan in a position where anything can happen. There's not going to be a stripper, there's not going to be any excessive drinking, there's just going to be a few friends and a good time. Don't worry, Zee isn't going to let anything like that happen. And I don't think Ryan wants it to happen either. He actually told Zee that he wanted something low key."

"Wow, I am impressed," Melissa said, arching her eyebrows. Then they relaxed into the spa treatment and enjoyed themselves without having to worry about anything going wrong. There had already been enough drama to last them a lifetime, and for now they just wanted the wedding to be plain sailing.

***

When the wedding day arrived Melissa was a bundle of nerves and emotion. She was so afraid of crying because she didn't want her make up to run, but it was hopeless because she couldn't stop the tears from flowing. John had been in contact with Zee during the morning to ensure that the preparation for the wedding was going off without a hitch, but they had been separated just as Melissa and Ryan had. The night before the wedding had been lovely. John and Melissa had taken a trip down memory lane, reflecting on all the years that had led them to this moment. It was a wonderful tribute to their friendship, and John couldn't deny that he was getting emotional as well. He dabbed his eyes, as proud as anyone could have been. Melissa looked utterly gorgeous in her dress as well, so radiant that he couldn't imagine anyone being more beautiful. He was just glad that if he ever got married he wouldn't have to compete with such a dress.

They were driven to the hotel in a sleek black car. The hotel had been decorated in a traditional way, but there were flourishes of color here and there to add a modern twist, as well as unusual and exotic flowers that weren't often seen at weddings. This was the compromise that Melissa and Ryan had come to in order to satisfy their differing desires when it came to the aesthetics of the wedding. John helped Melissa step out of the car and they walked into the hotel as string music played. The song was a modern one, again something that Ryan had requested, but the blend of the modern with the traditional worked perfectly, and it was a testament to their relationship that they had been able to pull these two things together.

When they entered all eyes turned to them and there were hushed murmurs at the appearance of Melissa. John's gaze darted straight toward the head of the aisle where Ryan and Zee were standing, awaiting the bride. Ryan's face was a picture of desire and disbelief that he was the one Melissa was walking toward. John's gaze drifted to his best man though, to Zee, the one who made his heart sing and his body dance with delight. Zee looked so handsome in his suit. He had trimmed his beard and made sure that he looked the best he ever had. But it was more than his appearance that had changed. The air of gloom around him had been dispelled, and John was proud of the part he had played in this. The rest of the world was a vast place, but it did not need to influence their lives here. Zee didn't need to feel as though he was going to be hurt again. John certainly didn't intend to hurt him.

As he walked up the aisle behind Melissa, John felt as though he was walking up toward Zee. It didn't feel wrong. He flashed Zee a warm smile as he approached. All he wanted was to go up to Zee and embrace him joyfully, to share a kiss and stand beside him. That would have to wait though, as John had to flank Melissa.

The officiant led Melissa and Ryan through the vows. Everyone's attention was rapt and the air trembled with emotion as Melissa and Ryan stumbled through their vows. John's lips trembled and his eyes were wet as he listened to them professing their love for each other. Whatever misgivings he had had about the wedding and the groom were dispelled entirely. Seeing them there together, pledging their lives to each other, it was clear that they were meant to be together. To see them together was a thing of beauty and John knew that even though they might have their troubles, they were always going to find happiness within each other.

When they finally said, "I do" and they kissed the crowd cheered and there was much joyous celebration. Finally John was able to go up to Zee and clasp hands with him. They kissed too and let the waves of happiness wash over them as the wedding continued into the celebration.

***

John watched with pride as Zee stood up to make his toast. The toast had been shrouded in secrecy. John had begged Zee to give him some snippets, but Zee had refused entirely. It was much anticipated, and John strained his ears to ensure that he did not miss a word.

"So I looked up how to write a good best man speech and most of the advice was to start off with a joke, but when I sat down to write one it didn't feel quite right, and then I decided that I was going to speak from the heart. I've known Ryan since we were kids. We've known each other for so many years that I can't remember a time when we didn't know each other. Our friendship started because we used to play with the same toys and we liked the same cartoons, but over the years its grown into something that has been defined by the experiences we shared together. Ryan has been there through my weakest times and pulled me back up. He's the kind of friend that wouldn't let me wallow in misery. He's the kind of friend that will come by my side and push me back into the light. I know sometimes this can make him a little difficult to deal with because sometimes you just

96

need to be alone, but Melissa I know that if you two do have an argument or a problem then he's not going to let it fester. He's going to want to sort it out and get things back to the way they should be.

For those of you who don't know, I left home to go traveling for a number of years. As a result I have only gotten to know Melissa recently, but she's definitely the best woman that Ryan could have ended up with. I was there at the beginning when he first learned about romance. At the time he said that he was never going to get married because he couldn't understand why anyone would settle for one woman when there are so many more out there, but that was before he met the woman that was better for him than any other. We've all had our share of heartbreak. I know I have, but being in your presence makes me believe in love again. Melissa, I want to thank you for making my best friend happy.

This is a happy occasion, so I'm not going to bring the mood down too much, but one of the reasons why I came home is because my father died. I never got to say goodbye to him. Ryan helped me through it. One of the things I learned on my travels is that family is the most important things in the world. Even though I was on a different continent, I wasn't alone, because I still had my family in my heart. And over the years I've learned that family isn't just the people you're related to, it's the people who care about you and who are there for you. Ryan is my family, and now Melissa is as well. You two are lucky to have found each other, but you make everyone you know lucky as well, because we get to share in your lives."

There was a soft ripple of applause and John wiped tears away from his eyes.

"I just want to say that this day has been very special. When I came back from traveling around the world I wasn't really sure what I would find when I came home. I didn't know if people would look at me the same way or if would even belong again. Ryan made it feel as though I hadn't been away at all. We picked up right where we left off and that's just the kind of man he is. He makes people feel better. I've seen a lot of things during my travels, but I've never seen two people more suited to each other. So here's to you Ryan and Melissa. You are one of the wonders of the world to me."

The toast was met with raucous applause and John noticed that Melissa was crying. Ryan went up to give Zee a hug, and then Zee came over to give John a kiss. John was proud of his man, and he was glad that Zee had been inspired to love rather than to wallow in misery.

***

The day settled into the evening. After the speeches had been made and the food had been eaten music began playing. The wedding cake was cut, and then it was time for the first dance. Ryan and Melissa took to the floor. John and Zee stood with their arms around each other, watching their friends enjoy their first dance.

"This is beautiful, isn't it?" John whispered to Zee as Melissa and Ryan began swaying to the music.

"It really is. It looks as though they belong together. And I think we deserve a pat on the back as well for getting them this far," he said with a twinkle in his eye. John laughed.

"You know," Zee continued, "I think people will say the same about us when they see us together."

"You do?" John asked, his face lighting up.

Zee nodded. "Melissa and Ryan aren't the only couple I think are the perfect examples of love, I just thought it would be a bit egotistical to namecheck myself in my toast," he said with a smile. John laughed and grabbed his hand, pulling Zee onto the dance floor when they were invited to join the bride and groom. Soon enough the dance floor was filled with other people who joined in, but John was blind to them all. He only had eyes for Zee. He draped his arms around the slightly taller man and closed his eyes, enjoying the closeness and the intimacy. It came so easily and so naturally to him now that he wondered how he had ever lived without it at all. Zee was such an important part of him that he was a part of John's own essence. It was as though he had not been complete until Zee had come along, and now he didn't have to worry about ever being away from him again.

The celebrations were joyous and it was one of the best nights of John's life. He celebrated with Melissa, Ryan, Zee, and all of the other guests. Before the wedding there was a part of him that had been afraid he would have felt sorrowful that his friendship with Melissa was changing, but on the contrary he had nothing but happiness for her. When he reflected upon this he felt that a large part of this was because he now had something important in his own life.

***

The night died down and people began to leave. Ryan and Melissa ascended to their honeymoon suite at the earliest opportunity to enjoy all the delights that the first night of marriage offered. John and Zee weren't far behind. They were tired, but were not in the mood for bed yet. However, they were hot and sweaty. As soon as they got into the room they flung their jackets away and unbuttoned their shirts.

"I don't think I'm ever going to get tired of that sight," Zee said as he gazed at John in his underwear.

"Then how about this one?" John said as he whisked his underwear off and stood in the room as naked as the day he was born. Zee smiled with hunger in his eyes. "I'm going to have a quick shower if you want to join me," John sauntered off to the bathroom where he turned on the shower. The warm water cascaded out of the shower and steam quickly filled the room, and he only had to wait moments before Zee joined him.

As John stepped inside he let the water hit his body. It trickled down in a frothing cascade, covering every inch of him in its comforting embrace. He closed his eyes and let it fall, and then he smiled when he felt Zee's presence around him. Hands ran around his waist. Lips were pressed against the nape of his neck. Teasing breaths were carried on the droplets of water. John felt himself melting into Zee. The hard, muscular body was surprisingly comfortable. Their skin pressed together and it was easy to get lost in each other.

John turned around and wrapped his arms around Zee's neck. He rolled forward on his tiptoes and drowned in a long, languorous kiss. Zee murmured with delight and pressed John against the wall of the shower. The coolness of the tiles contrasted with the heat of the water. The steam enveloped their bodies, but their hands searched where their eyes could not reach and they found each other's arousal. The kisses became more frantic as lips crashed together. Tongues danced. Occasionally clear water dripped in, invading their mouths. They spluttered and laughed as they stepped back and took in the sheer delight of each other's naked body. John ran his hand down Zee's chest and then grabbed some shower gel. He squeezed a dollop into his hand and then rubbed it together, creating a foamy froth. Then he started to rub it over Zee's body. Zee smiled. Over the past few months they had grown so close to each other that they knew each other's secret spots. John rubbed him slowly and lovingly. Zee put some shower gel into his own hand and started to wash John as well. They gave each other soft kisses in this most intimate places, letting the foamy soap trickle down their bodies, covering their manly flesh. A fresh scent filled the air around them as the water continued to pour. It was so warm neither of them wanted to move, but then there were other more comfortable places to be, places to which their desire would carry them.

Zee reached behind John and turned the faucet off. The water suddenly stopped. The stream went silent. Only trickling drips remained. Zee led him out of the shower and they pulled fluffy, huge towels off a rack. Zee wrapped one around John's shoulders and started to dry him. The towel was soft, but it was Zee's embrace that was more comforting and loving. Water trickled down their bodies, making the hair appear darker and thicker as it clustered together. As they dried each other they kissed. Both of them were erect and eager, their bodies responding in a primal way. The damp towels were left in a mess on the floor as they made their way back to the bed. Flecks of water still beaded on their hair and left damp shadows on the bed, but this coolness helped to offset the heat that emanated from them.

They lay against each other, legs entwining, hands roaming, lips locked in an endless kiss that was only broken by their moans. They drowned in each other's lust and sank into the softness of the bed. Their hands clasped together and tightened as the pleasure coursed through their bodies. They pleasured each other with their mouths, and every inch of their bodies shuddered with erotic delight. Hearts thrummed and their blood sang with desire as they sank deeper and deeper into each other. All John knew is that he wanted Zee more than anything in the world. The first time they made love had been electric, but each time since then had been more and more intense as the physical act was imbued with an ethereal spiritual energy that added to everything John was experiencing.

There were times when he felt as though he was floating and other times when he felt like he might faint. Sweat beaded on his temples and his skin became flushed as the passion swam through him, building up into an inferno inside. Zee knew how to touch him in the right way. He knew just how to caress and suck to elicit the perfect amount of pleasure, and John always felt as though he was in heaven whenever he was with Zee. It was incredible and left him breathless, and he wondered if anyone had ever been more satisfied or more fulfilled than he was.

Zee towered above him, his body so impressive, the perfect embodiment of masculinity. His erection stood out, so large and thick and John fell in love with it all over again. Zee parted John's legs and John watched as Zee plunged himself inside John. The sensation was a blurring of pleasure and pain, but what followed was a sweet satisfaction. John's body writhed and his neck arched as he braced himself against the feeling of Zee slamming inside him. Every muscle in Zee's body was tensed and focused on one thing and one thing only; John.

John's body rocked with every thrust. The rhythm played havoc within his mind and the sensations were almost unbearable. His vision blurred. All he saw was a god before him, a god crashing into him again and again, getting harder and faster as he gave into his animalistic side. John was twisting, his neck lolling from one side to the other as he felt the pressure building up inside him. Zee gripped John's cock while he thrust, and there was only so much John could take before he was going to explode. His moans were breathless, his body felt as though it was going to crack open like an egg. Everything was so rampant inside him and then it flowed out, gushing like the torrent of water in the shower. It was thick and wet and hot, swimming all over his stomach and Zee's hand. The sight of it was obviously enough to send Zee over the edge as well, because within moments Zee came as well. It was a roaring fury that drove him. His body doubled over and John's eyes went wide, for Zee had never gotten this deep into him before. The sensations were a crashing eruption and so intense, followed by a moment of silence as they sank into the bliss of each other's arms.

They laughed with each other, saying that they should have waited to have a shower because they had just made a mess of each other. But neither of them minded really. John's mind sizzled with happiness and he almost couldn't believe that this had happened to him. There was a time when he believed he was going to end up alone, and he was glad he was wrong. He almost felt as though he was dreaming, but if he was dreaming he knew that it was a dream he was not going to wake from, and he knew he was with a man that he never wanted to be apart from. They snuggled up together in each other's arms and thought about the future that was going to greet

them. It was going to be filled with happiness, and
neither of them could wait for it to begin.

Epilogue

Zee stood on the shore of the beach, looking out across the water. The beach was calm at this time of the morning. Very few people were around, and those who were kept their distance, respecting each other's privacy. Zee's life had changed a lot. It had been months since the wedding. In that time he had a collection of photographs published that had been very successful, and the publisher had quickly commissioned a second volume in the series. He and John had moved in together, finding a home near the beach that offered a wonderful view. Melissa and Ryan's marriage had gone from strength to strength, and they were now trying for a baby. Once they were successful Zee and John were automatic choices for the godfather of course.

But Zee often came here to look out at the horizon. In his youth his life had been built around the idea of leaving home to search for pastures new, and then he had left. He had explored the far corners of the world and in the end the only love he found had hurt him. He felt stupid now for being so tied to what he had experienced elsewhere. It was strange really, before he always used to feel the pull of the horizon, the lure of the next adventure, but now he didn't. He had never realized that there were plenty of adventures to experience at home, and now he wondered if he would ever travel again.

He spared a thought for Adam as well. The man had meant the world to him once, but now when he thought about him there was nothing but a hole in Zee's heart, as though the whole thing didn't mean anything at all. In fact he pitied Adam. The man wandered the world in search of something he was never going to find, always turning his back on the people who could have offered him love. It had been Zee's mistake to let himself fall prey to the man's charisma. Thankfully he had been able to break free before it had been too late, although it was only because his father had died.

He wished his father was here now. There was so much he wanted to tell him. But instead only the ocean was able to bear witness to his words.

"Dad, I'm sorry that I didn't realize what was important in life before I left. I thought the answers were out there somewhere. I didn't realize they were here all along. I shouldn't have been so stubborn. But I want you to know that I'm happy in every sense of the word. I've met someone special to me. I think you would have liked him. He keeps me grounded and he's not afraid to call me out when I let my emotions get the better of me. In fact he's so special I think I'm going to ask him to marry me," as Zee said this he put his hand in his pocket and felt the box he had bought. He pulled it out and opened it, revealing a shiny golden ring that gleamed in the sun.

"I don't know how you felt when you asked Mom to marry you, but I'm really nervous. I just... I hope that wherever you are you're proud of me and you're glad that I grew out of whatever drove me to leave this place. I'm sorry that I wasn't here to say goodbye to you. I wish that things had been different, but yeah... I just want you to know that I'm happy, and thank you for raising me the way you did."

There was more he wished he could say, but his words were lost to choking emotion. He closed the box and breathed deeply as he gazed out to the horizon. Then he turned away to go back home and prepare for the biggest night of his life, because it was the night when he wanted to lay down roots. This time if things went to plan Ryan would be his best man, and he had no doubt that Melissa would be John's best woman. The world still held so many adventures and so many unknown places, but he was happy to let other people explore them. The heart was the true undiscovered country, and he wasn't going to rest until he had traversed every part of John's heart. He turned his back to the horizon and left the world for someone else. He was going home to the man he loved to ask him if he wanted to spend their lives together.

There was no picture that could capture that kind of love, but Zee had finally found what he had been searching for all along. And now he was never going to let it go.